Praise for *Ezra and the Great Bin* … *en*

"Highly imaginative and full of ad… *Great Bin Jah Meen* is simultane… is a hero you can't help but … story is a complete deligh…

- Michael Leali, aw… *…he Civil War of Amos Abernathy* … *…out Triangles*

"Stevens has crafted an absolut… packed with heart, humor, and plenty of adventure. What more could you ask for? Both a deeply felt story about adoption and a zany caper to a magical land, it's so easy to love this book. And it's even easier to love Ezra, who will inspire the hero in you as he discovers the one in himself."

- Benjamin Roesch, award-winning author of *Blowin' My Mind Like a Summer Breeze*

"A beautifully told story that captures the sensitivities and difficulties of understanding adoption, as well as the challenges of ADHD, from the perspective of an eleven-year-old boy. We need more stories like this that adopted and neurodiverse children can read and relate to and enjoy."

- Miranda Mercado Gregory, co-founder of adoption support community *We Are Family* (WAF)

"A whimsical, fun, and emotional ride that shows how kids with all kinds of differences can be heroes. Ezra's exciting adventure toward self-acceptance and belonging carries the reader through new worlds that teach us valuable lessons along the way too."

- Jen Woodrum, Therapist and author of *The Severed Fates* series

"Stevens magically captures the joys and complexities of neurodivergence of the brave and bold (but not always feeling so) Ezra. This heartfelt tale is both entertaining and moving, and leaves the reader basking in a glow as golden as the jelly bit of a jaffa cake."

- Charlotte Pascal, SENDCo and ADHD mum

"A wonderful portal fantasy in the spirit of *The Phantom Tollbooth*. In *Ezra and the Great Bin Jah Meen*, an adopted boy struggling with his sense of belonging and isolation finds himself an unlikely hero, in an unlikely place against the last enemy he ever expected. A wonderful, imaginative book full of compelling characters, places, struggles and victories."

- Sarena Straus, Benjamin Franklin and Pencraft award-winning author of the *ReInception Trilogy*

"*Ezra and the Great Bin Jah Meen* is a beautiful book. Telling the sometimes tricky and definitely not straightforward story of a boy who feels 'elsewhere'. Ezra finds his inner hero on a boring Thursday thanks to the wonderful world of Sahs, cakes, trains and castles. This book covers difficult topics including adoption, loss of a loved one and family dynamics with humour, reality and empathy."

- Dr Elyse Waites, Pastoral Deputy Head Teacher

"R. D. Stevens has built a world with interesting characters you wish were your friends. Ezra has ADHD, and young readers can see the powerful feelings and contrast of scattered thoughts and hyper focus associated with this condition. Readers who enjoy adventurous fantasy stories will like *Ezra and The Great Bin Jah Meen*."

-Reader's Favourite, Five Stars

Enjoy the adventure!

Ezra and the Great Bin Jah Meen

R. D. Stevens

Illustrations by Juliette Caron

Dreamsphere Books
Winnipeg, Canada

Editor: Craig Gibb
Proofreaders: Sanford Larson

Published December 2024 by Dreamsphere Books.

Dreamsphere Books
PO Box 51053 Tyndall Park
Winnipeg, Manitoba R2X 3B0
Canada

Visit http://www.dreamspherebooks.com to find out more.

For anyone who has ever felt as though
they might be a little bit *elsewhere*.

Ezra and the Great Bin Jah Meen

Prologue

Begins With An Ending

Stories are everywhere.

They are in people, and on shelves, and across rooftops. They are on football fields, and in swimming pools, and under sofas. If you look carefully enough, they can be found in our tears, our tantrums, and our tragedies. And they can be felt in other's warm hugs, hard punches, and school lunches.

They explain the beginnings of the universe, and the lightning in the sky. And sometimes they're talked about by everyone, then lost forever when they die.

They can bury themselves deep into our memories and dreams, or shine on the surface of our chatter and beliefs. They are the invisible bindings that hold groups together, and the building blocks for barriers that keep them apart. They are the familiarity that floats between family and friends, and the feelings that linger when one's time finally ends.

People used to think that it was the gods that controlled our fates, but really it is stories that work their magic into our lives. It is stories that have existed since the beginning of time; they waited years before they could enter our dreams.

Lonely and untold, their magic gone cold, they lay dormant just begging for something to hold. And once humans arrived with their story-shaped minds, they jumped for joy, because they were finally live. They embraced us, enthralled us, and carried us through the fantastic, the dark and the light. It is stories that have allowed us to survive for so long, evolving on this journey through time. After all, all of the past is hi*story*, you see, so it's clear where they've been all our lives.

And stories, dear reader, don't like to be alone; they seek companionship wherever it may be found. They have a unique way of existing within things, planting their feet firmly onto the ground. It is their magical nature that does this. They are the glue that connects our pieces and parts. Each one of us is a patchwork of stories, you see, every scrap of cloth threads through our hearts.

If some of these scraps are not connected so well, the missing threads can leave us feeling a bit out of our shell. Because stories don't like to be left incomplete, they beg to be told and bring parts to a whole. They have the power to make us feel like we are *here,* if we can just stitch a pattern into the pieces that's clear.

And if there's a need that's there because a patchwork is bare, then from time to time the stars do their bidding to align. Of course, you may never see it, but the magic is real when those disparate threads intertwine.

Somewhere in the world right now a story is ending and another beginning, whilst others are still stuck in the middle. This story begins with an ending and a boy—Ezra Ben Castle of 23 Somerset Drive, Peckham, to be precise—who feels like he is existing elsewhere in this life.

Ezra is the hero of our tale, and a remarkable one at that, but at the moment we begin on a Thursday afternoon when he has returned home from school and dumped his rucksack in the hall, he wasn't feeling particularly heroic at all, and more like he was just in a good old fashioned bad mood. Some threads of his patchwork, those that were there, had recently started to wear thin and threadbare. And other threads were absent, location unknown, and this is what left him feeling alone.

Yet as chance would have it, on this particular Thursday afternoon, the stories of the universe were listening. As the stars aligned in the grey afternoon sky, and the constellations connected two worlds from up high, they were about to spin some new threads that were missing.

So, I will tread carefully in sharing this story with you, because it's a delicate new stitch in a patchwork still new. Pay attention, dear reader, as the magic ensues, for sometimes it's not obvious when it's making its moves.

Now then, let's begin...

Chapter 1

There Really Is Nothing Whatsoever To Look Forward To At All

Sitting down on the stairs with a thump, Ezra Ben Castle took off his battered black primary school shoes for the last time.

'Hi, honey, hope you had a good day?' called out his mum. 'Summer holidays are here! Hooray!'

She appeared from the kitchen wearing a flour dusted apron and a big wide smile.

'We've got lots to look forward to,' she beamed.

As he fiddled with the fraying laces on his faded shoes, Ezra sighed deeply. Right then, he wasn't looking forward to the summer holidays *at all.*

Six weeks off school and six weeks away from teachers and all the telling off and sitting down and silly things they ask you to do, that's no bad thing. But six weeks of doing different stuff at different times with different people—most of them grownups—well, that's all rather annoying and difficult in a whole other way.

But that wasn't his only problem.

Ezra had now finished year six (as of about half an hour ago), so he wasn't ever going to be able to go back to his school again even if he wanted to. And the fate that awaited him a few short weeks away (the dreaded *whisper it quietly* *secondary school*) meant that this summer felt to him like the beginning of a very slow, gruesome execution.

Everyone in his class had been at the end of term leaving party that afternoon. The other kids were running around and talking loudly and signing each other's shirts and squealing with excitement, but Ezra had been hiding round the corner by the book nook. Ever since he joined the school in year two, that had been his favourite spot.

They had spent the morning writing stories entitled *My Journey So Far* and, as if there weren't enough talk about their big *life changing transition* already, they'd even had an assembly about it and been paraded in front of the younger year groups. To make it even worse, each departing child's name was read out as they walked onto stage, and when it was Ezra's turn the Headteacher paused, frowned, and squinted at the handwritten list on her clipboard, before reading out '*Something* Benjamin Castle' which meant that half the school laughed as Ezra shuffled on stage and shrunk into his seat.

It felt to Ezra like all the teachers and kids spent the whole day reminding him about how primary school was finished, and why this was a very important life moment, and where he would be going next. He was going to have to start at *that* school in September which basically meant his number was almost up as far as he was concerned.

Oak Mount Secondary School for Boys was, from what Ezra could work out, a cross between a prison, a zoo, and a live torture experiment. Never mind all the new rules and hefty homework and ridiculous uniform and changing lessons and different teachers and changeover bells and five-storey buildings. As if they weren't enough, all the kids from his old school who thought he was weird were going there too, which was very not ideal from his point of view.

Add in the fact that weather forecasters were saying that this summer was going to be the wettest on record (which meant hardly any time for football in the garden) and the Castle family weren't going on holiday because they couldn't afford to, then, *no*, Ezra thought, *there really is nothing whatsoever to look forward to at all.*

Mum tried to give him a hug as he chucked his shoes on the rack, but he wriggled out of the way just in time. Mum, or Abby Castle if you want to know her real name (or Abby Valentine if you want to know her *real* real name before the whole marriage to Dad thing), was always trying to give Ezra hugs but almost exclusively never succeeding.

'Leave me alone, Mum,' he said, frowning.

Ezra walked past Mum into the kitchen and sat down at the breakfast bar, his head slumping onto his arms.

'What shall we do this afternoon?' asked Mum, following Ezra in and closing the door behind her.

'I don't know,' Ezra mumbled, the words getting lost in his sleeves.

'How about we play a game?' asked Mum with her eyebrows raised as she dusted down her apron.

Ezra groaned.

'How about Downforce?' she asked enthusiastically.

'No,' replied Ezra without moving his head.

'Cluedo?'

'Nope.'

'Rush Hour?'

'No…'

Mum paused for a moment and searched the air with her eyes as if looking for an idea. 'I know…' she continued. 'Ghost Hunters?'

'No! Mum, I don't want to play a stupid game!' he snapped, his feelings bubbling up and bursting out all of a sudden. 'I just really don't feel like it right now, okay?'

'Okay, okay,' replied Mum with a puff of her cheeks.

'I'm just trying to help, Ezra. I can see that you're not feeling good. I wondered if maybe a distraction might—'

'Well, it won't! Not unless playing a board game can magically cancel the summer and everything after it and put me somewhere else entirely…'

The kitchen door opened and a man walked in holding out his hands with a smile. 'Summer holidays!' he announced.

Mum shot the man a death stare but he didn't register it in time before continuing: 'How great is that?'

This man is Dad. Dad is not the hero of our story, but might be best described as an actor in a supporting role, like Mum. Of course, I'm not suggesting he is only acting as Ezra's Dad rather that he is not the focus of this unravelling. Naturally, Ezra's Dad believes that he is the hero of his own story (don't we all?) but I am not telling the story of Jim Castle, I'm telling the story of Ezra Castle. I can't tell two stories at once; it would simply be too confusing.

Dad stood there with his arms open wide, but it was as if they were holding a piece of silence up to the room because everyone looked at them and immediately said nothing.

'Ezra's feeling a bit upset right now and I'm not sure why,' Mum said, finally allowing Dad's arms to drop.

'I see…' replied Dad. 'Not sure what we're upset about. It's the first day of the summer holidays, right? School's out for summer, and all that! I used to love the excitement of starting school holidays.'

Ezra rolled his eyes.

'And you've got year seven to come in September!' Dad continued. 'Finally made it to the big leagues!'

Mum gave Dad another death stare when he said that, which he saw this time, but Ezra still didn't catch. Ezra often missed stuff like that.

Dad tried to ruffle Ezra's hair, but his hand was promptly swatted away.

'Maybe Ezra's just feeling a bit worried about all the change happening this summer,' Mum wondered, hopefully. 'Maybe if we sit down and try to plan it out a bit, that'll help everyone feel a bit better? I made a nice Victoria sponge earlier today,' she added, reaching for a flowery tin and opening it to reveal the beautiful golden cake inside, a thick trail of strawberry jam oozing gently out from its middle. 'How about I get the pen and paper so we can write out a holiday timetable, and, Dad, you get us each a piece of this and some juice?'

Ezra smelt the unrivalled buttery sweet vanilla smell of a fresh homemade cake and realised out of nowhere that he was quite thirsty, ravishingly hungry, and very tired indeed.

Chapter 2

A Big Swirl And Fizz

Ezra was glancing over the summer timetable that they had just made. It was quite beautiful, he had to admit. Mum took great care over the details, using a ruler and highlighters, and colour coded everything by week, event, and who was going with Ezra to what. Seeing it laid out like this, Ezra conceded that maybe there were at least a few things to look forward to like sleepovers at Granny and Gramps' house, and visiting the animal handling centre, and baking sessions with Mum if the weather was bad, even if it did only pave the way for his painful September demise.

Ezra put the lids back on the pens, finished his juice and walked over to the fridge to get some more. On his way past the countertop, he noticed the post tray sitting next to the cake tin. There were a couple of new envelopes there that he didn't recognise, and when he saw them a different part of his brain fired up and made him start wondering. Wondering can be a wondrous thing, dear reader, but is not always wonderful if you're not feeling so wonderful yourself when you do it. Ezra's brain often started wondering about things that didn't always make him feel wonderful, and he never really knew why.

Should I ask? he thought. It had been a long time since he had, mainly because he was afraid of the answer. He was still feeling a bit mixed up after that morning, and before he had the chance to properly decide, a question popped out of his mouth by itself.

'Have we had any contact letters this year yet?' he said as he flicked through the post that sat in the tray.

Mum and Dad's shoulders dropped at the table, and they both took a simultaneous slow, deep breath.

'Still nothing yet, dear,' Mum replied, gripping onto her glass. 'We're waiting to hear anything back, but…well, we might not get anything this year. We did talk about this, remember?'

'We didn't get anything last year, or the year before that either,' said Ezra. His voice was unusually quiet as he continued to sift through the contents of the tray.

'I'm sorry, sweetie,' said Mum, scraping the chair back behind her and standing up. 'I wish there were better news.'

'We haven't even had anything from Abraham?' he

asked, returning the letters to the tray and tightening his fingers around his glass.

'No,' replied Dad. 'You know that social services aren't sure exactly where his new family is now.'

'Why can't they just find out where they live and go and ask them?'

'Because it doesn't work like that, honey,' said Mum. She smiled a fragile smile that felt like it might break.

'Well, it should. And birth mums should have to write to their birth children and their letters should come every year, that's what letterbox contact *means*! What's the point of having it set up if the letters don't come?'

Ezra's voice was becoming more agitated and all those bottled-up feelings from earlier were starting to mix together in a big swirl and fizz to the surface.

'We send ours to the social workers every year, Ezra,' replied Mum. 'We always write about you and what you've been up to. I don't know if birth mum reads them, but they are there for collection if they want to. That's as much as we can do. I'm sorry, I know it's disappointi—'

'No, you don't! You don't know it's disappointing, how could you? You never got removed from your birth parents! You never had to write about your *life journey* and not know what to say! You weren't adopted so how do you know?' Ezra was scowling, the hurt flowing through his voice, and his knuckles whitening.

'Ezra,' said Dad, standing slowly with his hands out in front of him. 'Let's calm down, shall we? I know you're upset about this, but maybe now's not the time to—'

'Then when is the time? There's never a time! You always say that! If you helped me, we could find my birth mum and ask her for a letter. Why don't you do that?'

'Ezra, you know we can't do that,' said Mum before quietly walking over to Ezra. 'Come here, why don't we go and watch something?'

'No! I wish I was anywhere else but here!' Ezra yelled. He shook Mum's hand off his shoulder and, before even he knew what he was doing, launched his glass at the slate floor. When he let go, he watched the receptacle fly through the air as if it were in slow motion, spotting his reflection in its surface as it fell. He almost didn't recognise the face of pure anger that stared back at him before it cracked, split, and smashed on the tiles. Mum and Dad leapt out the way and the glass shattered into a thousand tiny shards, the pieces scattering all over the kitchen in a brilliant burst of bright rainbow light.

'I don't want to *come here*!' he shouted, reeling from the crash and flash of light that felt as if it had somehow reached his insides. 'Why would I? You never want to help me! You don't understand. I've had enough of this stupid family!'

'Ezra!' shouted Dad. 'That's enough! Go to your room!'

Chapter 3

Boulders In The Hallway

You might have figured out by now, dear reader, that Ezra's dad isn't his birth dad nor his mum his birth mum. By which I mean, Ezra was adopted when he was little because his birth parents couldn't look after him. He had to be removed by social services to keep him safe and was put into foster care before being adopted by Mum and Dad a year or so later. Ezra has not met his birth parents since, and has lots of difficult feelings about this which he'd rather not have, but Mum and Dad always tried to tell him as he was growing up that whoever's tummy you come out of doesn't make any difference to the family in which you belong.

When Ezra was little he would repeat those words as if he understood them, but over the last few years he has grown up a bit and had lots more questions about his life story, which haven't always been easy, or possible, for Mum and Dad to answer. The contact letters that his birth mum could send each year via social services stopped coming. His birth mum had another child—Abraham—which he also doesn't hear from, even though Ezra, Mum, and Dad wrote to their adopted family every year too.

Sometimes when he has thought about it, it has made him cross and sad and frustrated and confused all at once. Dad always tried to remind Ezra that being a Mum and Dad is about what you do, not whose genes you've got, and Parker didn't come out of Mum's tummy either (as Mum was also keen to point out) and he was just as much a member of the family as anyone else. Ezra accepted that some of the time, but wasn't always convinced, especially when he wasn't feeling wonderful already, as was the case at this point in our story.

'Why do I have to go to my room? It's not fair!' he yelled.

The kitchen door slammed and Ezra's feet stomped their way upstairs.

'You are always making me annoyed, Dad! Why can't you just stop?'

A bedroom door slammed this time followed by the sound of a box of toys being tipped onto the floor. Ezra threw open his wardrobe and looked for something else to launch.

'Sometimes parents have to do things that their

children find annoying! It's my job!' yelled the loud, irritated voice of the just-about-middle-aged man that was Dad holding a dustpan and brush.

'No, it isn't! It is not your job!'

'Yes, it is! It is my job to look after you, keep you safe and help you to grow up. And that means doing things sometimes that you don't like. Like sending you to your room when there's glass all over the floor!'

Dad was now holding onto the bannisters with one hand and looking up the stairs past the rubber plant on the landing at a closed door. This is Ezra's room. There is a sign on the door which says *Privat Prop ertee! Keep out!*

'I can look after myself. It's my body so it's my rules; you can't tell me what to do with my own body!'

'I can if you're using your body to smash things! And I will because you are eleven years old and not old enough to look after yourself!'

'Aargh!'

There was a sound of another box of something or other crashing onto the floor.

'You are only going to have to tidy that up later, young man!' yelled Dad.

'No, I'm not! This is my room, so it's my property, so I can do with it what I want!'

'You still have to tidy it up!'

'NO, I DON'T!'

This was not the first time that a conversation like this had happened in the Castle family home. In fact, something like this had occurred at least once or twice a week for the last year.

Mum was now sitting in the living room trying to read a book. She doesn't like it when people shout, especially when it is the other two members of her family hollering at each other from opposite ends of the staircase. Again.

Mum started trying to read a book entitled *Emotions and How to Manage Them* and was determined to find the answer within. She had a habit of buying books and reading them to find out answers. The funny thing is that any time she seemed to find an answer, it just brought about more new questions and so she bought more books to try and answer those. I'm not sure how many answers there are out there, dear reader, but sometimes it seems like there are rather a lot and at other times it seems like there aren't any at all. It's all quite disconcerting.

'Will you keep it down up there, please!' she said, in her slightly-louder-than-normal voice that suggested she was annoyed but not enough to stop reading her book.

Ezra heard her but pretended not to. He was breathing fast and heavy and surveying the mess he had just made. He cursed his Dad under his breath with a word that he heard at school and didn't know the meaning of but was sure was a swear. Another boy in his class, Curtis, said it and he had a whole bunch of rude gestures that he taught the class every break time so Ezra thought he must know what he was talking about. As soon as the words left his mouth, he knew he shouldn't have said them, and listened out for a moment, worried that someone might have heard.

At times like this, Ezra felt like no one ever understands him and the whole world wants him to be unhappy. Just then, he was really angry about something, he knew it, but his mind was going a million miles an hour and he couldn't remember what. And then, after he finished checking no one heard his swear, *Oh, look!* he thought. *There's my Harry Kane card, I haven't seen that in ages!* He knelt down to pick it up from underneath the pile of Lego that had been tipped on the floor and looked for the rest of his football card collection. It seemed to him like a good time to start creating a team made only of players that have an H in their name.

Ezra's brain worked so fast sometimes that even he forgot what he was thinking about. Mum and Dad have shown him a collection of books about his fast brain (Mum has lots of them) and how it works a bit differently to many other people's. There's even a fancy grown up name for how fast his brain goes with a bunch of letters he can never remember the meaning of. There's definitely an A for attention, but he doesn't know what the D and the H in the middle stand for. However, he does remember what the final D, the one that ties it all together, means: disorder.

He doesn't understand why the D would stand for that when, surely, as he pointed out to Mum one day, 'It should just stand for difference, shouldn't it? It's just a bit faster than other people's, and is wired up differently, it's not *disordered.* It's not like my brain doesn't have any order to it, it's just arranged in a different way and what's wrong with that? It's different, that's all. Saying it's dis-ordered, sounds like it got lost in the post or someone sent it back.'

After Ezra said this, Mum had agreed and got a tissue out of her pocket for some reason. She had then tried to give Ezra a hug, which he hated, before he got more cross about grown up decisions and disorder and chucked all those books about his super-powered brain into the recycling bin. Of course, they magically appeared on his bookshelf again later that day, but Ezra didn't notice.

Once he finished arranging his best lineup of players with H in the name—*Marc Guehi, Tyrick Mitchell, Michael Olise, Harry Kane, Harry Maguire, Hector Bellerin, Harvey Barnes, Son Heung-Min, Mo Salah, Erling Haaland* and *Kasper Schmeichel* in a pretty killer 4-5-1 formation—Ezra stood up and stretched out his back like a cat before wondering what he was going to do next. It was then that a loud clattering *clap* of a metal pan dropping to the floor downstairs made him jump out his skin. For a moment, it was as if time stood still as everything went silent. Stepping over the toys that were scattered across the floor, and opening his door just a crack, he carefully put his ear in the gap to try and hear what was going on.

'How did it happen?' his Mum was asking. Dad wasn't answering so Ezra figured that she must be on the phone. Along with her voice was the sound of muffled sniffs and sobs. *She's crying*, Ezra thought.

He knew that sometimes Mum cried when she was sad, and other times when she was happy. But sometimes Ezra just found her crying and Mum pretended that she wasn't, and he didn't know why she was crying at all. At those times, she got red blotches on her cheeks and put on a soft smile that disappeared a bit too quickly before changing the subject and usually suggesting they play a game or do something that made Ezra sigh. He doesn't like board games because no one ever follows the rules as they're supposed to, especially when they play Monopoly.

Ezra crawled further out of his room and listened carefully through a gap in the bannisters, trying to figure out what type of crying his Mum was doing on this occasion.

'I don't understand you, Dad, slow down…' *Mum must be on the phone to Gramps*, he thought. 'Slow down, slow down! Where is she now? Mmm hmm. Okay, how much longer do they think she has? What? That can't be right. Have you asked for a second opinion? Look, I'm coming now. Have you called Marcy? No, no, it's okay. I'm coming now. I'll call her on the way.'

There was a jingle-jangle in the key pot and Ezra heard Mum's coat being pulled on. A bustle of bags and shoes suddenly stopped and all there was was silence. Ezra carefully peered down the stairs and saw his Mum, her head hanging down and one hand over her eyes. Her back was shaking up and down and Ezra recognised that type of crying.

Mum was sad.

Dad appeared next to Mum and wrapped his arms around her and they both stood there hunched over like boulders in the hallway. She rubbed her hands across her face and glanced up the stairs to see Ezra looking down.

'What's wrong?' Ezra asked.

'It's nothing, sweetheart. I've just got to go and see Gramps,' Mum said. Of course, she was lying, and even Ezra could tell this, but she sniffed loudly and hurried out the porch door before he had a chance to ask anything else.

Dad invited Ezra back downstairs and put on a film for them to watch but didn't see any of it because he was up and down on the phone all evening. He kept putting his phone to his ear, lurching up off the sofa and pulling the kitchen door too so that Ezra couldn't hear. Ezra was watching the film (the animated *Aladdin*, one of his favourites) and didn't hear any of what Dad was saying, so the words 'heart attack' and 'how long does she have' and 'should I try and get there now?' fell quietly to the kitchen floor.

They got takeaway pizza for dinner, which made Ezra put his powers of deduction into overdrive. They hardly ever got takeaway anymore, not since Dad took his new job which meant that they all had to 'tighten their belts', as he called it. Ezra never understood that phrase. *How can you tighten your belt if you never wear one?* Anyway, he knew something must be up because of the pizza thing, and he was allowed to eat it in the living room in front of the TV which almost *never* happened, so that put him on edge even more.

After he had finished his favourite barbecue chicken pizza, he put the box in the kitchen and found Dad staring at his phone again.

'When's Mummy coming home?' he asked.

Dad swallowed loudly and sniffed before turning towards Ezra. 'Probably not tonight, buddy,' he replied. 'Best to start getting ready for bed, eh?'

'What's going on?'

Dad took his glasses off and placed his fingers on his eyelids. 'Granny's not very well,' he said, his voice quiet and deliberate.

'What do you mean? What's wrong with her?'

'We can talk about this in the morning, okay?' Dad

ruffled Ezra's hair. He hated when his Dad did that. 'It's time for bed. You've taken your tablets?'

'Yes, but…I don't want to go to bed 'til Mummy gets back. I'm not tired. And, who'll read my stories?'

'I'll do it tonight.'

'But…'

'Come on, Ezra. Please, can we not argue tonight? You just need to get ready for bed so we can get some sleep. We're all tired.'

Ezra knew something was wrong and he didn't feel right, but he also knew something was wrong with Dad which got him really worried so he did what he asked. After brushing his teeth and getting ready for bed, Dad came up to read him a chapter of his latest book (a rip-roaring adventure set in the deserts of Ancient Egypt with pharaohs and tombs and mummies and cursed treasure) before switching on the hallway's night light and heading back downstairs.

It took Ezra over an hour to fall asleep. He played with his toy soldier collection for a bit and then, in the sliver of light from the hallway, read his *Minecraft* annual for the umpteenth time. Later, whilst he was fast asleep and snoring, his mum returned. She walked in through the front door and when Dad approached, dropped her knees to the floor. Dad crouched down to hold her and they both began to cry.

'I can't believe she's gone,' she said, sobbing deeply. 'It's all happened so fast, it doesn't feel real.' She sniffed, wiping her nose with a tissue as she looked up to Dad. 'How are we going to tell Ezra?'

Chapter 4

Lightning Doesn't Flash In Circles

Ezra rested his head on his hands and stared blankly out the window. *Why do these things have to happen? And why do they happen to me? It's not fair,* he thought as he scratched his cheek.

Rain drops slowly trickled down the windowpane and grey clouds filled the sky outside. He watched as a puddle of water grew on the roof of his climbing frame. Leaning forward, he tried to spot the robin's nest in the ivy that clung to the fence running along the back of the garden, but it was hard to see any details in the bad weather. He couldn't even play football when it rained like this. The grass goes all boggy and makes the ball stick in the mud so it lands with a *splat*.

Granny liked football. She used to play in a women's team back when women were barely even allowed to have a kickabout. She always had a great story about how they had to fight to play and everyone laughed when she told them that she was in a team. All the boys used to laugh, she said, *Until I took it round them all, 'megged the defender and scored top bins, then they stopped!* Ezra smiled at the memory of her face. When she spoke about her glory days playing football, there was a sparkle in her eye and a grin that made everyone else around her happy.

It had been a week since his Dad told Ezra the news. *Heart attack*, he had said. *Sometimes these things just happen.* Mum had been busy since that Thursday, always on the phone or out meeting people. Ezra had been at home mostly with his Dad. Sophie from next door had been over a couple of times to babysit, but no one else had come to the house.

Ezra had been unusually quiet, too scared to argue or ask anyone what was going on. He didn't really understand what had happened, he just knew that his Granny was gone and now everything seemed different.

Ezra thought of when he used to play with his Granny in the garden, teaming up to take on Dad, and how she would pretend not to know the garden football rules so that they would always win. Everyone knew if the ball landed in the flowerbed then it was a throw-in, but she would always kick it away just as Dad got there and get Ezra to play on, claiming she had forgotten. She would blame it on being an *old codger* and wink at Ezra after he had slotted the ball home and wheeled away in celebration.

Ezra was staring at the flowerbed in his garden as the memory played out like a film in his mind, when all of a sudden there was a blinding flash of light right where Granny once kicked the ball out of Dad's hands. Ezra sat bolt upright and pressed his face against the windowpane. Had he imagined it? Mum and Dad often said he had an overactive imagination, which he didn't believe for one minute. *But big brilliant bright white flashes of light don't usually happen in the garden*, he thought. And he was not wrong about that.

Just as he started to think maybe there was a storm and it was just a flash of lightning, there it was again! It was even bigger this time; a crackling, sparkling circle of light that flashed flickers of colour like a firework. *Lightning doesn't flash in circles!* he thought as this time the light stayed there, pulsing and swirling right on top of the flowerbed. It began to spin vertically like a disc, turning faster and faster and sending out more and more sparks until it was moving so quickly that it was a beautiful whizzing blur. Ezra leapt up and opened the window, leaning out to get a better look. His arm got soaked from the rain as he pushed the window wide, and with a better view he really couldn't believe his eyes. *What is going on?*

'Mum!' he yelled. There was no reply. 'Mum!' he tried again. 'Something weird is happening in the garden!'

He ran out of his room and opened the door into his parents' bedroom. Mum was lying curled up in a ball under the duvet again. He'd found her there a few times over the last few days. She looked small in her position, wrapped up like a tiny baby, her arms clinging around her middle.

'Mum!' Ezra said. 'Something's happening in the garden!'

'Mmm hmm,' mumbled Mum. 'I'm trying to rest, Ezra. Please, just give me a minute.'

'Seriously! I'm not making this up! Something's on the flowerbed; a kind of light and it's moving really fast.'

'Oh, Ezra. It's probably just a reflection or something. The weather's bad today, maybe it's the storm? Please, let me have some quiet time. I need to get some rest. Mummy's very tired.'

'But, Mum—'

'Ezra, please,' Mum interjected, turning away from him and burying her head in the covers. 'Go and look if you really need to find out what's there.'

Ezra sighed loudly and huffed in exasperation. *Why doesn't she listen? Adults always take the wrong things too seriously*, he thought. This was important and all she could do was roll over and ignore him.

'Fine. If you're not going to, I'll go and look,' he announced curtly before turning with purpose and marching downstairs.

When he got into the living room, he peeled the curtains just a crack to see if the strange occurrence was still there and, sure enough, the spinning circle of light was burning as bright as before. Parker joined him at the door and stared out with a quizzical look on his face. This is the moment, dear reader, that it is time to properly introduce another hero of our story.

Parker is a dog.

A miniature schnauzer, to be precise. He has grey fur, a white-tinged brown moustache, and inquisitive eyes that make him look like a cross between a teddy bear and a grumpy old man. Parker is fearless and scrappy and spirited and wise, unless he is around cats or foxes or bubbles, in which case he forgets all sense and is none of these things all at once.

'I know, Parker, I know,' said Ezra, his eyes fixed on the strange patterns of light. Parker started to whine and paw at the door as he always did when he wanted to go outside. 'Okay, boy, let's go and take a look,' Ezra continued, turning to fetch his coat and shoes from by the front door.

Zipped up and comfortably covered from the rain by his hood, Ezra carefully turned the key in the back door, took a deep breath, and stepped out. In amongst the patter and splatter of the rain, was a sound he had never heard before. It could best be described as a crackling hum; a throbbing, buzzy sound that was emanating from the light. It was like he could hear the power and energy coming from it. Ezra edged closer to the flowerbed, taking careful steps and holding onto Parker's harness for security. Parker wasn't barking, which he always did at any ordinary intruder in the garden, like a squirrel or a bird, so Ezra thought this must be something entirely different.

He approached the shed that sits next to the flowerbed

and leant against it, feeling the warmth coming from the light. He tentatively began to peer closer, and it was as if the swirling vortex were magnetic, drawing in his gaze with the colours and light reaching into infinity. He was about to reach out a hand to try and touch it, when there was a loud *crackle* and *bang* and the circle of light instantly grew as tall as the garden fence. Ezra leapt out of the way just in time because the very next moment, you wouldn't believe it, but a train began hurtling out of the spinning portal at full tilt.

Chapter 5

The Cream Before The Jam

Rolling over onto his knees, Ezra couldn't believe his eyes as an old-fashioned steam train with an engine, a coal truck and a single carriage in tow burst into his garden. It had a deep green coloured water tank with thin red stripes, a black chimney and cast-iron buffers. He had seen something similar when he visited an old steam railway with his Dad years ago, except this was less than half the size of anything he had seen that day. Every feature was exactly in proportion, it was just all significantly smaller. The whole thing stood no higher than Ezra's shoulders and the column of steam that rose from its chimney was the width of the washing-line pole that the train narrowly avoided as it careened forward.

No sooner than it had burst into the garden, there was a loud screech of the brakes that made Ezra cover his ears.

The train's wheels stopped moving and it slowed to a halt just before it crashed into the petunias that were next to Mum and Dad's favourite fence. *Phew*, thought Ezra. There would have been big trouble if the fence had come down, it was practically brand new. *How would I have explained that?*

A big puff of steam burst into the air out of the chimney and the pistons sighed, creating a white, billowing cloud that surrounded the engine. Ezra grabbed a hold of two handfuls of grass and crouched there frozen for a minute not knowing what to do. What *do* you do when a miniature steam train drives out of a spinning disc of white light into your garden on a Thursday morning just before lunchtime? Exactly—I wouldn't know either.

As he sat frozen on the wet grass, the warmth of the train's firebox made its way over to him and he was glad of its glow. Ezra, listening intently, waited to see what would happen next, and after what felt like ages, he heard the sound of some tiny voices coming from the engine cabin. The steam disappeared into the air as the tiny voices began to have what sounded a lot like the beginnings of an argument.

'Are you sure you put the settings in correctly?' said one tiny voice, high pitched and squeaky.

'Yes, of course, I did!' replied the other. This one was a little deeper and more hoarse, as if it had a bad cold. 'I put exactly the right number of raisins into the scone before I baked it.'

'And you remembered the flour?'

'Of course, I remembered the flour!'

'And the eggs…?' The high-pitched voice was getting higher with each concerned question.

'And the eggs. And the sugar, And the milk,' came another hoarse, defiant reply.

'And the butter?'

'Yes! All the ingredients were there.'

'And you made it just how he likes it?'

'Yes, Emily!'

'Well, something's not right. Hang on,' the voice Ezra now knew belonged to an Emily paused dramatically before continuing. 'You did put the jam on before the cream, right?'

'The jam on befo… Wait. The cream goes on before the jam, doesn't it?'

'Tell me you didn't… No!' There was a sharp intake of breath followed by a high-pitched groan.

'Yes, it does! Why would you put the jam on first? That doesn't make any sense!' bemoaned the other character Ezra now understood to be called Percival.

'Oh, Percival! That's not how it works! You put the cream before the jam? No wonder we've ended up somewhere different. It's jam first, then cream!'

'Since when?!'

'Since the Great Bin Jah Meen said we need to make scones to use the depot! Since he dictated the new rules for driving a train in!'

'Oh, pancakes!' sighed Percival. 'No one told me! You know it's my first day on the rails with these new-fangled portal things, you should have said something! If we're not at the depot, then where are we, Emily?'

'I don't know. No one has ever put the cream on before

the jam before…goodness knows where we've ended up. What are we going to do?'

'I'll…I'll take a look. Hopefully we aren't too far away. We can probably just turn around and go back. Shivering sherbets, Emily, we are going to be in so much trouble!'

Ezra looked at the train intently and saw a pink nose surrounded by a set of slender, grey whiskers peek out from one of the engine cab windows. As the nose wiggled and sniffed the surroundings, a pair of blue eyes soon followed with it, and Ezra could then see a whole face. And what a strange little face it was.

The piercing blue eyes and pink nose sat above a tight-lipped mouth with big white front teeth, all of which were surrounded by a short coat of soft grey fur. Above this, two floppy triangular shaped ears pointed out from either side of a coal-stained train driver's cap. Ezra had never seen anything like it. He thought that it reminded him a little of a mouse or one of his school gerbils that he took home to look after last Easter, but it had human-type features and was clearly standing up and talking. As the bright eyes cast about looking for something recognisable, they caught sight of Ezra and widened in shock. The head disappeared instantly back into the driver's cab along with the sound of a sharp intake of breath. The voices started again.

'Er, Emily. There's a…a creature out there.'

'What kind of creature?'

'I don't know… It's big and sort of olivey brown. And tall. And looks a bit like us, only with smaller ears. And no fur.'

'No fur?! What the eccles?!' There was a pause. 'What shall we do?' continued Emily, her voice trembling.

'I don't know! What if it wants to eat us?'

'To eat us! Crepes! Surely not? Why would it want that? Did it see you?'

'Yes, it saw me!'

'Well, it hasn't tried to eat us yet, so maybe it's not hungry? How many more scones do we have left?'

Percival checked his pockets. 'Two: one for elevenses and one for emergencies.'

'Alright, well, why don't we try and give it one of our scones, as a sort of…gesture? Maybe it won't eat us then and we can get this train turned around and head back?' Emily asked, trying to muster up some positivity in her voice.

'Okay, okay. Fine. You take the scone out then.'

'Me? Why should I do it? You got us into this pavlova, you should do it!'

'Oh…'

Ezra could hear some squeaking and a few snuffles before another sharp intake of breath. 'Fine,' Percival continued, 'I will. But if it eats me, then it's your fault! Now, where's that scone? Ah, here it is. Okay, alright. If my Mum ever wakes up, tell her I love her. Phew…I'm going for it!'

The door of the little engine cab opened ever so slowly on the side where Ezra was sitting and a tiny, polished black boot gingerly stepped out onto the footplate. Ezra leaned forward to try and see inside the cab, but the creature—who Ezra knew now was called Percival—slipped out and closed the door tightly behind him, only giving Ezra a brief glimpse at the other being inside. Percival hopped delicately down off the footplate and nervously opened up a gingham tea towel.

'Hello?' Percival said, timidly. 'Would you like a scone?'

Chapter 6

Did He Just Say Wednesday?

Ezra carefully edged forward so he was on all fours, making sure he had good footing in case he needed to run away.

'Are you real?' he asked, tilting his head as he caught sight of a feverishly twitching fluffy tail poking out the back of Percival's overalls.

'What do you mean?' replied Percival, curtly.

'I mean, you're not just imaginary? My Mum says I imagine things sometimes and, well, this is all pretty unusual so I'm wondering if I'm imagining you.'

Percival looked down and stared at the scone for a moment. 'Well, I don't know,' he replied. 'How do you know if you're only imaginary? I don't *feel* imaginary, if that counts. But I've never felt any different, so how am I supposed to know if that's not just what feeling imaginary feels like?'

Percival sighed. He turned round to look back and shrugged his shoulders at Emily. Emily nodded toward the scone again.

Percival glanced to the side for a minute, as if to catch a thought that was trying to escape out of his ear, before turning back to face Ezra. 'How do I know that *you're* not imaginary?' he asked Ezra with a newfound confidence in his voice.

'Well…' replied Ezra, pausing to examine his hands. 'My Mum thinks I'm real, so…I must be. Look…if I think you're real and you think I'm real then that should be enough to rule out any of this business about being imaginary, okay? Let's shake on it.'

Ezra extended his hand toward Percival and held it outstretched in the air. His Dad had taught him that people like to shake on things if they are agreeing on something that isn't a proper rule; it's one of those things that makes no sense but everyone just knows what it means somehow. Unless you're Ezra and you need your Dad to figure it out for you, of course.

Percival narrowly eyed the blank space in front of him as if he were lost deep in thought. Then with a twitch of his tail, and a tweak of his whiskers, his shoulders lightened, and he thrust out a paw.

'Deal!' he exclaimed, and the furry palm of his little paw

disappeared inside Ezra's grip. Ezra felt its soft, warm fur and decided he must be real if he can touch him.

'Why did you need scones to get the train in here?' Ezra asked. He was beginning to feel a little less scared and a lot more curious.

'Well, what's the fastest cake in the world?' replied Percival.

'I don't know.'

Percival rolled his eyes. 'A *scone*, obviously. Sponges! Don't you know anything? What are you, anyway?' he asked, eyeing Ezra up and down with a twitch of his tiny nose.

'What do you mean, what am I? I'm a person,' said Ezra indignantly. 'I should be the one asking you that question, driving a train into my back garden unannounced. Are you some kind of gerbil?'

'Gerbil?! A gerbil?! You persons obviously don't know very much! We are Sahs, and we are certainly not gerbils! How rude!'

'We really need to return to the depot, Percival,' interjected Emily, daring to lean out the train's cabin. 'It's nearlymost time for when we were supposed to be dropping off the rails already.'

'Oh crumbs, is it? We are going to be in real trouble, friend!'

'What's the depot?' interjected Ezra, not sure what was going on.

'What does he mean, what's the depot?' asked Percival looking at Emily. 'Doesn't he know?'

Emily shrugged and rolled her eyes.

'It's the only depot you take the train to,' Percival continued, turning to Ezra. 'You know, the imagination depot where everyone gets all the materials the Great Bin Jah Meen requests.'

'Who is the Great Bin Jah Meen?'

'Crepes! Who is the Great Bin Jah Meen?!' Percival's eyebrows raised and he snorted. 'Where have you been living these last Thursdays, under a scone?'

'I'm sorry,' Ezra replied feeling more and more confused, 'I've just never heard that name before. And, sorry again, but did you say these last *Thursdays*?'

'What day is it today?' Percival asked Ezra, pointedly.

'Thursday,' he replied.

'Precisely!' he nodded his furry little head. 'And what day was it yesterday? Thu…'

'Wednesday,' interjected Ezra.

Emily and Percival stared at each other before retreating slowly into a huddle next to the train. 'Did he just say Wednesday?' Percival whispered, incredulous.

'Yes, I believe he certainlymost did,' whispered Emily back. 'Do you think he is feeling alright? Should I check?'

'Yes, maybe you should.'

Emily cleared her throat and turned back to Ezra, who, standing in the rain only two feet away, had heard all of their conversation. 'Are you feeling alright?'

'Well, I have a sore knee but my Mum says that's just growing pains. Otherwise, yes, I think so. I'm not really sure why you're asking,' replied Ezra.

'Only,' Emily scratched her nose, 'you seemed to say that yesterday was Wednesday.'

Ezra frowned. 'Because it *was* Wednesday. Today is Thursday, yesterday was Wednesday and tomorrow will be Friday. That's how a week *works*,' he said, rolling his eyes this time.

Percival and Emily inhaled sharply in unison. 'Are you saying,' Emily forced out, 'that you're not stuck on Thursday?'

Ezra laughed. 'No! Why would we be stuck on Thursdays?! That doesn't make any sense!'

Percival had to hold onto Emily's shoulder to steady himself before replying. 'Because, since the Great Bin Jah Meen arrived, it's been one long Thursday! It never ends; we go to sleep on a Thursday and wake up and it's still Thursday. And then we go to sleep again and wake up and it's Thursday some more. He appeared on Thursday in a shower of glass shards from the sky—the great, most mysterious *Shattering*—but it wasn't until later in the day when the thunderous *Clap* struck that the world stood still. The hours pass but the sun stays high in the sky. It never sets for a new day. We never get that Friday feeling, we never have a weekend, we never have our cakes on hump day, it's just always Thursday. Are you telling me that is not happening here for you persons?'

'No, that is definitely not happening here!'

Emily's eyes flashed open wide. 'Then we must be somewhere the Great One doesn't control! We must have gone to somewhere outside of the power of his Heka. Wait…what were you imagining when you spread that scone, Percival?'

'I was…I was imagining the same thing I do most of the time: going somewhere else. Somewhere…away. A new story where we weren't just stuck imagining train track and building more railroads into the Desert.'

'That must be what happened! You imagined a different place and somehow the backward scone allowed the depot to create a way to take us there!' Emily looked intensely at Ezra. 'Where are we, exactly?'

'Well, this is South East London,' Ezra replied. 'But my address is Somerset Drive, Peckham.'

'Summasetdurivepeck-ham. Wow!' exclaimed Percival. 'Are you anywhere near the Desert of Apep?'

'Um, there are no deserts in London.'

'Mmm, the Great Lake of Shenou?'

'Er, we've got a pond in the park down the road, but I don't think that counts as a lake.'

'What about the beaches at Wahed?'

'No,' laughed Ezra, 'there's no beaches around here. I wish there were!'

'Well, crumbs!' exclaimed Percival. 'Hold on, you're not anywhere near the Sa Mines are you?'

Percival and Emily both leaned in to hear Ezra's response. 'There's pretty much only towns around here, no mines,' said Ezra. The Sahs' shoulders dropped at Ezra's reply. 'Where are all these places?' he continued, feeling very confused.

'What do you mean, where are they? Have you never heard of them?'

'No. I've heard of Peckham and East Dulwich and Brockley and Tulse Hill and all that, but nothing like what you're talking about.'

Emily's tiny hand shot up to her mouth. 'You mean, none of those places are here at all?'

'No!'

'Well, golly gosh and great scones! We really must be outside of Ankh Bah!' Both furry noses turned to each other with smiles spreading across their faces. 'This is it,' said Emily as they nodded to each other, 'this is our way to stop the Great One!'

She turned back to face the newfound person creature

standing in front of her. 'Ezra,' she declared, 'you're big, maybe even as big as Bin Jah Meen. Will you come and help us?'

'Wait—where is Ankh Bah?' Ezra asked, frowning.

'It's where we live! You live in Summasetdurivepeckham, we live in Ankh Bah.'

'Well, I've never heard of Ankh Bah,' Ezra shook his head. 'It's definitely not in South East London.'

He sighed and wondered what on earth was going on. *How is any of this possible?* The Sah duo continued to look at him with depths of expectation in their eyes, it was almost too much to bear.

'Help you do what?' he finally asked reluctantly.

'Help end his rule! Help us escape the power of his Heka and restore our ibs! Help us get out of Thursday!'

'Well,' Ezra replied, thinking of the time and hesitantly looking back at the house. It was eleven o'clock on what had, at least until this point, been a very ordinary, boring Thursday morning. Nothing happened at home these last few days. His Dad was back at work and his Mum was upstairs resting again.

She wouldn't believe me even if I tried to tell her what was going on, he thought, *and no one would miss me*. He was fed up with being stuck at home whilst everyone else kept on arriving and leaving, keeping him out of whatever grown up stuff was happening. Why shouldn't he go somewhere different? *No one wants me around here at the moment anyway*, he thought. He eyed up the steam train. It was an impressive piece of machinery and he'd always wanted to go for a ride in one.

'I have absolutely no idea what any of that means,' he announced, 'but I've got about an hour before lunch so I guess I could give it a go?'

'Huzzah!' squeaked Percival and Emily in unison. 'Right then, let's go!'

Chapter 7

Mums Are Quite Often Right About These Kinds Of Things

Ezra climbed into the empty truck that was being pulled by the engine and sat down facing the rear. It was a squeeze, but with his knees curled up and shoulders squashed he just about fitted in. There was a loud clunk from the engine cabin and he turned to see Percival stick his tiny head out the window just before a massive dump of steam filled the air around him. The train lurched and then slowly began to inch backward toward the spinning swirling light.

Of course, Ezra thought, realising that he was going to be at the front of this journey into the unknown, *it's on a track so it can't turn around*. As Ezra edged closer and looked down at the ground before him, he realised he could begin to see the other side. The train track flickered into view and appeared to stretch out as far as he could see across an arid, moon-like landscape.

'Wait,' said Ezra. A sudden feeling of fear and anxiety had entered his mind. 'Where exactly are we going?'

'We've got to cross the Desert of Apep before we can get back to Ankh Bah. Keep your arms inside the carriage,' said Percival sternly, 'we're going through the gate!'

Ezra quickly wrapped his hands around his middle, shut his eyes and held on tight as he could feel the warmth of the flashing light around him. The hairs on his arms rose and he felt as if his skin was shining, fizzing and bursting all at the same time. Somewhere, he could hear Parker's barking but he wasn't able to register it in amongst the sensory overload that engulfed him. As he continued to move forward, the warmth of the gate was abruptly replaced by the thick, hot air of a desert.

He opened his eyes a fraction before quickly shutting them again because of the glare from the rays of a new blazing, unforgiving sun. As he blinked his eyes into adjustment, he was gradually able to twist his head and take in the enormity of the desert that surrounded him. The stark landscape stretched to the horizon in all directions, desolate expanses of beige sand occasionally interrupted by eerie rock formations or spherical, bluish-grey bushes and nothing else. The heat rose off the sandy floor and made everything look as though it were floating.

Ezra turned around just in time to see the gate spark and speed up like a pinwheel firework before disappearing in a puff of smoke. As the smoke cleared, a tiny, oblong concrete building at the end of the tracks came into view. Emily pushed her head out the side of the train, her fur ruffling in the breeze.

'That's the imagination depot, in case you're wondering much,' she yelped at Ezra through the wind. 'We'll bring you back here after.'

Ezra wished he'd thought this through a bit more. His mum was always telling him to do that. And, well, dear reader, it should be noted here that mums are quite often right about these kinds of things. Quite often, at least…

'And you can get another gate up so I can go home again?' he asked, picking at the skin of his thumbnail.

'Begging your pardon?' shouted Emily.

'You can make another gate again when I need to go home?' he shouted.

'Oh yes, certainlymost. As long as we were right about the scone, cream, and jam situation, then we shouldn't have any troubles at all.'

'But what if it wasn't the scone thing? What if it was something else?' yelled Ezra.

'Well, then…' Emily ducked her head back in before reappearing moments later. 'Well, we are nearlymost certain about the scone thing, so that's our answer.' She offered

Ezra a thumbs up sign with her tiny pink mitts before disappearing into the cabin once more.

Great, thought Ezra, *these guys don't know what they're doing. What if I get stuck here?* He started to play out worst case scenarios in his head—slowly dying of thirst or getting eaten alive by vultures, for example—when he noticed something on the horizon and lost his train of thought. *What's that?*

Nestled within the vast desert expanse, as if it were sprinkled into the rugged beauty of the desert by the giant hand of an artist, was a collection of tents, woven intricately and adorned with vibrant patterns.

'That's Apep,' squeaked Percival in his loudest voice, pointing at the colourful dots ahead of them. 'Nearly there! Just you wait 'til everyone meets you. Hah! Great scones! It's going to be so fantabulous!'

Ezra swallowed hard and wished he'd remembered to bring Parker with him. He was a terrible guard dog, but at least he was brave and scrappy and good for cuddles and licks. And because Ezra wasn't feeling particularly courageous himself any longer, this was the kind of moment when a good dog cuddle was entirely needed.

Chapter 8

It Doesn't Even Have Any Fur!

The train's brakes screeched as the engine pulled into a tiny station consisting of a sole platform, a water tower, and a miniature wooden bench. Ezra climbed clumsily out onto the platform, which was a collection of tree stumps lined up next to each other, and stretched out his back. Emily hopped off and began busying herself with the hose of the water tank that sat atop a pylon next to the track. The train, like a parched desert wanderer finally reaching an oasis, began to gurgle down the liquid, swelling the tank once more and preparing it for its next trip.

Percival took his hat off and ran those little pink fingers through the fur on his head. 'Right,' he said, trying to sound confident. 'Let's go and see my parents. My Dad will know what to do with you. Come, come. This way,' he beckoned.

Ezra stepped off the tree stumps and followed Percival

down a dusty pathway that led in between the tents. Up close, the tents' geometric patterns and decorative stitching were wonderful. Made of woven hair or fur, they were a mixture of black, brown, beige and grey, with the occasional dash of dyed colour adding a touch of artistry to their otherwise practical design.

'Do you live here?' he asked.

'I live in the city, Ankh Bah. But my parents live here. I grew up here as a child. It used to be a bigger community, but many of us have moved away. No reason to move back now; there's nothing here for us anymore. Not now the Great Bin Jah Meen has arrived and closed down the depot for all but him.'

Stopping outside one of the tents, Percival took a deep breath and said quietly, 'Just so you know, my Mum has run out of ibs so she's not doing very well right now.'

Before Ezra had a chance to ask what ibs were, Percival pushed back the cloth of the tent door and ushered him inside. Ezra was forced to crouch down onto his hands and knees in order to squeeze through the entrance. The dark cool of the tent was a welcome break from the glaring sun outside and, after his eyes took a moment to adjust, Ezra examined the home that was laid out before him.

There was a pole in the centre of the tent and a small wood burning stove next to it with a crooked metal chimney that poked out through a hole in the roof. There were three small beds, including one which had someone curled up and buried under the patchwork covers, a porcelain wash station, a wooden dresser and chest of drawers, and a small table with four stools for seating. Perched on one of these stools was another of the furry creatures that Ezra now knew were called Sahs. This one, with grey fur and a thin frame, was busy sewing together a pair of trousers with needle and thread. When Ezra crawled in, he looked up and screamed.

'What the glazes is this?!' he yelled, jumping off his seat and grabbing a stool to arm himself. 'Get out of my home, you…you, whatever you are! Go on! Get out!'

'Papa, please! It's okay!' pleaded Percival.

'How is it okay?!' he yelled back. He was wafting the stool wildly in the air and even Emily was having to duck out the way. 'Look at the size of this thing! Get back, you monster! Get back!'

The greyer Sah advanced forward like a lion tamer, thrusting the stool in Ezra's direction with all his might. Ezra shuffled back as far as he could go (which wasn't very far considering his size) and put his hands up in surrender.

'Don't hurt me, please!' he cried with his eyes closed.

Just as his papa was about to poke Ezra with the stool, Percival leapt in front of him. 'Papa! Stop!' he shouted. 'He's our friend! He's here to help! To help us against the Great Bin Jah Meen.'

This caused Papa to pause for a moment. 'Help?' he said, with a confused look on his face. 'The last time anything this size came along, it was the Great Bin Jah Meen himself, and we all know how that has turned out! How do you know this, whatever it is, is here to help? It doesn't even have any fur!'

'Because he's from outside, Papa. We found him, and he certainlymost wasn't trying to come here. He didn't appear here, like the Great One, *we found him.*' Percival puffed out his chest as he directed an open hand in the direction of Ezra. 'This,' he announced in his best formal voice, 'is a *person*. And he is called Ezra.'

'A person?' said Papa, elongating out the word in his mouth as he said it. 'What the eccles is one of those?'

'Well…it's this,' Emily quietly chipped in. She gestured her pink fingers at Ezra, waving them in the air around his face. 'See? He lives in a place called Summasetdurivepeck-ham, and he's—'

'Never heard of it,' announced Papa with disdain. He was still gripping the stool tightly in an *en garde* position.

'Yes, well, neither had we until half an hour ago, but, well…the thing is, in Summasetdurivepeck-ham it's not Thursday all the time.'

Papa breathed in sharply and froze. 'Not always Thursday?' he said, turning to look at his son.

'Not always Thursday,' replied Percival, reaching out to take a hold of the stool his Papa was holding and slowly lowering it to the ground. 'Let me explain,' he said quietly.

At that point, Percival and Emily explained everything they had learnt so far on what had been the most remarkable of Thursdays in their whole lives. Ezra slowly relaxed out of his crouched position in the corner as the story unfolded, ending up cross-legged on the floor with his head bent forward under the roof. As the two Sahs finished their tale and waited with bated breath to see what Papa would do with this news, the old creature turned to Ezra with a look of wonder and trepidation.

'So,' he said, sitting back down and letting go of his

jousting stool before looking into Ezra's eyes for the first time, 'Ezra the person can help us?'

'I...I don't know,' muttered Ezra quietly, 'but I could try.'

Chapter 9

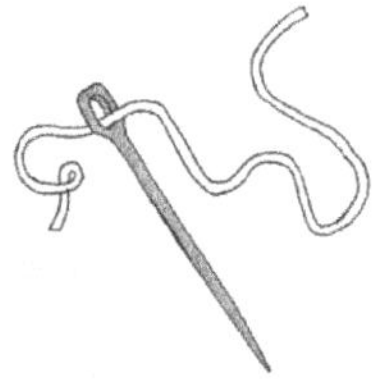

Thick And Sticky As A Toffee Apple

Papa was busying himself with the quilt and sheets that were on his wife's bed, tucking and untucking the corners until they were just how he wanted them. Ezra had been sitting quietly, trying to understand what Papa, Emily, and Percival had been explaining to him about all the problems that had started since the Great Bin Jah Meen (or Great One as Ezra noticed that they often called him) had arrived.

'As you can see,' Papa continued, 'my wife is very sick. She has no more ibs and is almost totally empty.'

Papa glanced up to see Ezra's look of confusion. 'No… more…ibs,' he pronounced slowly as if Ezra spoke a foreign language, but the boy's expression didn't change.

'Hold on a minute!' Papa exclaimed, a look of realisation crossing his face. 'Don't tell me you don't have ibs in Summasetdurivepack-ham?!'

'No...I'm afraid we don't,' said Ezra apologetically.

'Great scones! Don't you ever feel sad or angry or happy as a *person*?'

'Well, yes, some of the time. I mean, not usually all at once, but I do feel those things.'

'And where do these feelings come from?'

Ezra thought this was quite a strange question to be asked. 'I...I don't know, really. They sort of turn up in my mind after things happen or when I think about things.'

'But how do you top them up?'

'Um, they sort of do it on their own, I think.'

'They come from you? You create them yourself?' Papa's voice was filled with amazement.

'Well, I suppose so, yes, if you put it like that. Why? Don't you?'

'No! Our feelings grow from our ibs. We have to replenish them otherwise they run out.' Papa pointed to a large glass jar that was standing in the corner of the tent. It was empty but for a few drops at the bottom. Ezra's gaze was drawn to those droplets of water; it was as if they shimmered in the light.

'This is where we keep our ibs for drinking,' Papa said, walking over to the jar. 'We fetch water from the fountain in Ankh Bah and store it here. At least we used to before...'

'The ibs are in the water?' asked Ezra, scratching his head.

'Yes, they derive from the ib stones that are placed in the fountain. The stones are useless on their own—nothing more than plain old rocks—it is the fountain that brings the ibs to life. The ib stones originate from all different places but are brought together in careful quantities to build a harmonious mix in the fountain. Too much of one tips the balance, and it is a difficult balance to attain.

'Over many years, we Sahs have worked hard to make sure that the water for our ibs is in perfect harmony. The fountain is the source of all ibs: anger, greed, fear, sadness, compassion, hope…love, and all the rest. Ibs are the only thing that the Imagination Depot can't create. That and life, of course.

'We have to drink the water from the fountain so that we can restore our ibs and feel them when we need to. But since the Great One arrived, he shut down the fountain and its well. No one is allowed to access the well and so everyone's stores of ibs are running out. My wife is almost on empty,' he stroked his little hand across her head. 'You can see she has no feelings left. When we run out of ibs, we lose our ability to live.'

'I don't understand,' said Ezra. 'You can't feel anything without the ibs, and you can't get hold of them anymore?'

'Yes, we naturally run out of ibs when we are tired or run down, or things go wrong, so we need to keep them topped up from the fountain. But now we can't access them, we just run down until we have nothing left.'

'And what…' Ezra paused. He was almost too frightened to ask. 'What happens when you run out of ibs completely?'

'Then…' Papa hung his head. 'Then we die. Our souls can't survive without ibs. We need emotions to live, to breathe, to grow, to *fight*. The Great Bin Jah Meen doesn't understand this. He is an outsider like you. Ever since he arrived, he only wants everyone to feel one thing—despair—but no one knows why.'

'This is the reason he is making us build the train line all the way past the depot and into the Desert of Apep,' chipped in Emily.

'And why we were on the train to the depot today to get more track,' added Percival.

'Yes,' Papa continued, 'it is from the Desert that the ib stone of despair is derived. The Great One wants to find the stone of despair from out in the Desert, and as much of it as possible, and then fill the fountain with it so that it is the only ib available. That's why he's having this new railroad built. Once he has that built, he can send Sahs to dig for the despair stone in order to send it back on the cargo trains.

'No one knows how long it will take to find the stone, but it is believed that some parts of the Desert of Apep are filled with it, just under the surface. It's why, until now at least, nobody ever goes beyond Apep and the Imagination Depot. By the time he gets his hands on the stone and fills the fountain with it, well, it might already be too late…'

With a tear forming in his eye, Papa bowed his head and picked up his wife's hand. Emily looked up at Ezra and continued.

'On this neverending Thursday, the Great Bin Jah Meen built his castle on top of the fountain, banned all from entering it, and announced that he had removed the stones. He declared that he will open the fountain again once he has refilled it with the stone of despair. He knows that if we want to live, we must replenish our ibs so we need to find the stone. But if we do, and he fills the fountain with it, we will only be capable of this feeling for the rest of our lives. If he succeeds, we will despair forever. This, he must never be allowed to do.'

Ezra took a deep breath and let it all out slowly. 'Cripes,' he said in a slightly less than heroic fashion. 'That sounds awful.'

'Yes, certainlymost, it will be awful!' replied Emily. 'That's why you need to help us stop it, Ezra of Summaset-durivepeck-ham! You are the only one who can! We Sahs have tried, but no one can get near him.'

Ezra looked stunned. And terrified.

Emily, noticing this, hastily added in a much more

jovial voice, 'But you make your own ibs, so you'll be fine, yes!'

She laughed a laugh that was a little too loud and a lot too nervous, before clearing her throat and continuing. 'Will you pay him a visit, Ezra? Will you ask him to stop? Explain to him what we said to you and ask him to restore the fountain? No one else can do it, you see? He doesn't listen to any of us. You're the only one…'

There was a long pause and the air in the tent sat suspended, thick and sticky as a toffee apple. Everyone was glued to the silence, waiting for someone to take a bite and say something so that they could get unstuck.

Ezra stretched out his legs in front of him, making his knees click and nearly knocking over the dresser in the process. This was not what he was expecting when he got on that train, let alone when he went out into the garden on a wet, miserable Thursday morning. *Why am I here?* he thought. *There's nothing I can do to stop this; I can't fight despair. I'm just a kid. I'm not some kind of superhero.*

There are many things that Ezra has got right in our story so far but that time, dear reader, he was wrong.

With Percival and Emily's pleading faces, Papa's stern gaze, and the sight of Percival's mum buried under the blanket all adding to the stickiness in the tent, Ezra gave in and took a bite just to relieve the tension.

'Okay,' he said. 'Okay. I'll go. But I've got to be back by lunchtime, remember?'

'That is probably certainlymost excellent news!' squealed Percival. 'We must leave without any further ado-ing! We will stop on the way to see our friends in a bakery on the outskirts of Ankh Bah. They have glimpsed the Great Bin Jah Meen from afar. Maybe they can give you some tips...and a scone for fortitude, yes!'

Percival grinned and held two thumbs up in the air. Ezra tried a smile but, even in all the stickiness of the tent, it didn't stick around for long.

Chapter 10

History In The Baking

With the *clickety-clack* of the train wheels sounding out once more, Ezra sat up straight in his cargo truck as the buildings of Ankh Bah began to appear over the horizon. He wondered how long he had been with the Sahs. His Mum might have woken up by now and, if so, would probably have gone into his room to ask him what he wanted for lunch. When she realised he wasn't there, she would start to worry.

Abby Castle was an expert worrier, especially when something had gone missing, and Ezra knew that his Mum would be in, as she would say, *a right old state*, if he was the thing that she couldn't find. Sometimes, when his Dad got cross after Ezra had lost his temper, Ezra did wonder whether he would miss him quite as much as his Mum would, but when things cooled down, his Dad always tried to do something to show him they were alright again like offer a kick about in the garden or get out some Lego. *What if I never make it back?* wondered Ezra.

'How long will we be?' Ezra shouted back to the driver's cabin. 'Only, I should probably get home soon. We are just going to talk to him and then leave, right?'

'Yes, yes,' replied Emily, her whiskers waving in the wind. 'We'll take you to our friends at the bakery first for a quick visit, and then onto the castle. You'll be home in no time at all, I'm sure!'

Ezra faced forward again and breathed in sharply as the train began to enter the city of Ankh Bah. The buildings were all made of brick and clay and reached no more than two or three stories high. As the train track weaved and wended its way through the structures on either side of it, Ezra realised that nothing in this city was arranged in straight lines. It wasn't ordered like any town he had ever seen before. There were no roads he could identify and the pathways that existed between buildings only flashed briefly into visibility before disappearing again as they approached another house or wall or bakery (and there were a lot of these because, if you haven't figured it out by now, cakes are the Sahs only food group) in their way.

The train track climbed higher for a moment and he cast his eyes up the buildings and across the skyline. Smoke was pluming out of wonky chimneys, and the bristly, green canopies of stubby trees poked clumsily out between the buildings, interrupting the orange sea of tilted, tiled, terracotta roofs.

Windows were everywhere, some with little boxes of plants sprouting flourishes of colour and others with pastel curtains twitching in the breeze. There were no glass panes in any of the frames so the windows all remained open and Ezra couldn't help but peer inside, occasionally catching a glimpse of a Sah or family of Sahs inside. As they went about their days, he noticed their clothes, which were a wonderful collection of cotton garments; a weathered assortment of aged finery, all bearing the marks of time. Faded hues, frayed seams, and patches of discolouration told stories of countless washes and countless lives. They were all dressed very smartly, but nothing they wore was new.

The train turned another bend and slowed to a halt, a billowing cloud of white steam enveloping Ezra, Emily, and Percival as they climbed out and hopped onto the ground.

'This way,' called Emily.

Ezra followed her off the track and down a narrow, dusty alleyway. The buildings rose up above him on either side and, with his head just about the height of the first-floor windows, he could hear some faint gasps from their insides as he walked past. Ezra caught the eye of one little Sah who was staring at him with the utmost wonder, amazement, and awe. Unsure what to do, he offered a smile which made the tiny creature hop and skip with excitement.

After less than a minute's walking down the path, Emily came to a stop outside a double fronted shop. It had, written in peeling paint across the top of two open windows, the words: "The Rolling Pin—Roll Right In!"

Percival's nose twitched as he closed his eyes. 'You can't beat the smell of a good bakery!' he said, pausing as if in a trance.

'Right, we don't have much time,' Emily interjected.

'The Great One will be expecting us back from the depot. Come on, Percival, we need to go in.'

Emily pushed open the door and a tiny bell jangled somewhere in the back. 'After you, Ezra of Summaset-durivepeck-ham.'

Ezra walked in and was hit by a wave of warm, intoxicating, delicious air. A blend of sweet and buttery notes tickled his senses and took him somewhere else. With each breath he felt the smell drawing him further in, every inhalation deepening the connection between him and a scent that somehow smelt like home. He held the smell inside his lungs for a moment, closing his eyes just as Percival had done outside. The place smelt *right*.

'Okay, okay, what can I do you for, my salubrious Sahs?' came a voice appearing from a back room. 'We've only got scones as the Great One decreed but I've got a nice selection of ja… Woah!'

The Sah who approached the counter stopped suddenly and did a double take when he saw Ezra.

'Well, if this isn't more history in the baking, as if we haven't had enough of that lately! Greetings, Emily and Percival, what on earth have you two got yourselves into this time? Never in my key lime pie have I seen one of… What is that?' the Sah asked as he dusted down his paws and apron.

'Hello, Uncle Leopold. That is a *person*,' replied Emily.

After this announcement, Ezra looked over to see Emily smiling and appearing to be quite proud of her grand arrival.

'Is that so? Just when you think you've seen it all, you get a furless beanpole appear in your bakery. If this Thursday wasn't strange enough already.'

'He's going to talk to the Great Bin Jah Meen for us,' Percival added, puffing out his chest with pride. 'He's going to get him to let us use the fountain again.'

'I'm going to *try*,' said Ezra. He was starting to feel a bit uncomfortable with the expectations that now seemed to be falling upon him.

'Ah…well, good luck with that,' replied Uncle Leopold, taking off his apron to reveal a neatly tailored three-piece suit with a patched-up pinstripe pattern underneath. 'You're going to need it.'

Chapter 11

It Buries Into Your Bones

Uncle Leopold placed his apron neatly on the counter and walked out to inspect this new creature that was crouching before him. The bakery was small inside and, aside from the counter which was covered in scones, there wasn't much room for anything else other than the three adventurers, Leopold, and a single table with two chairs. Ezra noticed another empty ib jar in the corner like the one he saw in the tent earlier, and a strange big glass shard standing on the counter beside it. It had small bubbles in the glass, and Ezra felt sure he'd seen something like it before. *Don't we have glasses just like that?* he tried to recall, but felt too nervous to focus on the question.

'Hmmm,' Leopold murmured, circling around Ezra, examining him. 'Does this *person* have a name?'

'My name's Ezra,' answered Ezra diligently.

'Well, Ezra, you might be better off going back wherever you came from and forgetting all about this,' he announced, clicking his heels together as he came to a halt. 'I've seen the Great Bin Jah Meen and you don't look much like you'll stand a chance. His heka is too powerful, it shines out of him in shocking colours…'

'Heka?' Ezra asked. He was feeling confused and scared, and only a residue of *rightness* left from the smell was preventing him from panicking.

'Yes, heka!' Leopold peered at the blank expression on Ezra's face. 'Cinnamon buns! Tell me that persons have heka, they must do!'

'I would if I knew what it meant…' Ezra replied.

'Heka is his heka, it's his…' Leopold tapped a tiny paw on his nose. '…his magic, his *aura*. Everyone here has one. It sends out signals into the world without words. It emanates from within us and brings others into our ibs too. It is wonderful when our joy or happiness or enthusiasm is infected into others, it allows us to share the beauty of our inner feelings with others through the merest of smiles or looks.

'But when it is anger or sadness or despair, this can be hard to escape. Anger is when heka can be at its most powerful, pulling us into arguments and confrontation that we never intended to be in. I saw the Great Bin Jah Meen once, just as he arrived. That's where I got a piece of the

Shattering from. I retrieved it before the thunderous *Clap* that stopped the sun.'

He pointed to the shard of glass that stood on the counter.

'That and other pieces just like it rained down from the sky near the fountain the very same moment the Great One appeared. Just crashed to earth out the sky as if out of nowhere, and then there he was. Nobody knew what was going on. I was near the fountain at the time, going on a trip to get more water when it happened.

'Luckily, I was far enough away that he didn't see me, but as he got to his feet, I could feel his anger. He was glowing brilliant red, his heka somehow manifesting itself in the colour of its purest form. They say his colours change depending on his mood. Purple for despair. Red for anger. It nearly drew me in, even from my distance, but, luckily, I managed to run away just in time before his light could reach me. Some other Sahs were not so lucky,' he said, looking down sadly.

He straightened his suit before continuing. 'Those in his light haven't been seen since. It is said that the Great One's heka is so powerful when it touches you, it is like a vacuum sucking in all those around so that you cannot escape. His anger transfers to you as if it were your own. They say he glowed purple after the great *Clap*, and that his sadness sinks into you like you were grieving. And his despair...his despair is almighty heka at its worst.'

Emily leaned in toward Ezra and spoke in little more than a whisper. 'They say his despair is so powerful that it buries into your bones and you cannot tear it off. They say to meet him is to discover the emptiness of despair, and that it is worse than an emptiness of ibs. And without the fountain to replenish our hope and our balance, those who meet him sink so deep into their despair that they cannot be pulled out.'

Ezra lowered himself down onto his knees. Leopold sat at the table and Emily and Percival avoided each other's gaze. They shared their fear and even the smell of warm scones wasn't enough to save the mood.

'But you're bigger and stronger than us, yes?' Emily added, hopefully. 'And you can make your own ibs, remember? And you've never heard of heka, so maybe it won't even work on you! So, you'll be able to get yourself out, right? We Sahs can't do it, Ezra. That's why we need you to try.'

Uncle Leopold cast a quick glance at Emily's hopeful face and raised his eyebrows. Ezra missed the look, as he usually did with that kind of thing, and it was probably best he did, dear reader. He was feeling like a jumbled-up whirlpool of whipped everything when luckily another waft of warm cake smell hit his nostrils and sparked a thought that plucked him out of it.

'Scones were my granny's favourite cake,' he said, looking at the golden-brown pile of soft baked deliciousness sitting on the counter. 'She would always buy them for us in her local tearoom when I stayed with her and Gramps. They smelt just like this. They smelt *right*. I used to love spreading on the jam and then the cream inches thick, and taking that first bite that would get it all over my nose. Granny used to laugh every time before wiping it off with a napkin.

'She would sit quietly and listen whilst I ate my scone and talked to her, no matter what. She would just smile and nod and ask for an explanation if she needed one. In those moments, she always made me feel like…like I belonged. When we had demolished our scones, we would wash it all down with a cup of tea or an apple juice before going for a kickabout in the park.'

Ezra sighed and rubbed his nose.

'But she's gone now. I won't ever get to do that again,' he said quietly. 'Not with her.'

No one said anything as the warm smell weaved its magic and briefly transported each of them to their own memories of loved ones and laughter.

With a puff of his cheeks, Uncle Leopold stood up and delicately placed a paw on Ezra's knee.

'Perhaps I was too hasty,' he said, looking at Ezra with wisdom in his eyes. 'Maybe you are the person to save us. You know what it is like to lose something, something you can't get back, and I'm sorry that you have experienced this, but you know what will happen here if you don't try to help. You know how we will feel as we start to lose our grannies, and papas, and brothers, and mums. You understand despair and why we must not allow the Great One to succeed.'

Ezra sighed and nodded slowly, his eyes glistening.

'Because you know how this will make us feel, this gives you strength, *person*. Enough strength to take a trip into the castle and confront the Great Bin Jah Meen, yes? Your empathy for others, your love, this does not make you weak. This is the greatest strength of all.'

Leopold, Emily and Percival all looked at Ezra with the same expression as he inhaled the intoxicating smell once more and knew what he had to do. Ezra pushed himself back up to his feet.

'Okay,' he said, biting the skin of his lip. 'I'll give it a try.'

'That's the spirit! Roll right in, Ezra the person' said Uncle Leopold, sending a smile across the three adventurers. 'Roll right in!'

Chapter 12

The Growl Of A Great Beast Awakening

'They will be expecting us back from our trip to the depot, so we should be allowed in through the gates no problem.'

Emily was filling Ezra in on the final details as the steam train chuffed along the last leg of its journey. Ezra started to tap the toes of his left foot against the carriage side. Up and down. He did this as a trick to try to help him stay calm. Sometimes it worked, but today it didn't seem to be doing much good.

'Make sure the tarpaulin covers you all over, Ezra. If they see you there it could be a bit of a bun fight,' Emily added.

'What? Why? If who sees me?' Ezra asked, panicking.

'Well, as Uncle Leopold said, some Sahs fell under the Great One's heka when he first arrived. Those are the ones who weren't so lucky. They now work to protect him at the castle. They live at the castle in constant despair, so they say. I am thinking that they certainlymost won't be too impressed if you just walk up to them and ask to be let in, look at the size of you! And the Great Bin Jah Meen doesn't really like guests, especially not unexpected ones.'

'Thanks for letting me know!' said Ezra, sarcastically.

The train continued its journey through the metropolis and his toes started tapping faster.

Ezra noticed a hustle and bustle to the city as he peeked out from under his tarpaulin, but there was no traffic noise, no hums of office units or beeping alarms. No background of shouting or swearing or aeroplane engines. Instead, he could hear the patter of paws, the chatter of conversation, and an indescribable sound of what he could only describe as *general busyness*. And, as he saw each of the little creatures he passed scamper around, and gesticulate, and relate to each other, he suddenly realised something else was missing: no one had a phone. No one was staring at the palm of their hand whilst they walked, or listening to a video, or filming anything.

He wasn't allowed a phone yet (only being eleven years old as his parents pointed out to him) and he deemed this to be a great injustice, but to see that they didn't exist here was almost as startling to Ezra as the whiskers on their cheeks. This place felt entirely different to the city that he knew and had grown up in and, as he sunk back down into the train carriage, he suddenly felt a very long way from home.

The train turned a sharp bend and began to slow down as it approached a building that stood looming over the others. It was a castle made of grey stone which was at least twice as tall as any other building around. It towered above everything else, like a magnificent fortress from the past, built with thick stone walls that rose like giants out of the earth. It had four turrets, like watchful sentinels, that reached up into the sky from the four corners of the castle, and battlements across the top of the walls that sat between. Giant stained glass windows in ornate stone frames in the lower part of the castle gave way to narrow, dark arrow slits as the turrets stretched higher. A red and blue chequered flag flew from a pole in the far corner, and thick trails of smoke rose from a huge chimney.

Ezra couldn't help but be impressed. It was everything he imagined an old English castle to be.

'How old is this building?' he asked as quietly as he could now that they had slowed to a walking pace. He always enjoyed history lessons at school; he was enthralled by the Ancient Egyptians and amazed by the empire of the Incas. But he especially loved it when they learnt about the trebuchets and flaming arrows and boiling tar and battering rams and all the other gross ways to off people that were used in the sieges of castles in battles of the past. This year they had learnt about the English Civil War of the sixteen hundreds, and, as well as being a fascinating tale of power and greed, Ezra thought it delightfully gruesome too.

'It was only built at the start of Thursday when the Great Bin Jah Meen arrived. He made us get all the parts from the Imagination Depot before he closed it for anything other than train track. No one here ever imagined anything like this before so it's been a bit of a shock to say the least.'

The train approached a bridge that led over a small moat with the track's entry into the castle keep blocked by a huge portcullis gate. Ezra buried himself as best he could under the cover and held his breath whilst the brakes screeched and the engine hissed. When the hissing had died down, he listened carefully as Emily stepped from the train cabin and spoke to a guard who was standing bolt upright and in the uniform of what looked a lot like a Cavalier from the English Civil War, but not quite.

She had the plumed hat, adorned with a white feather, and an elaborate fitted, waist-length jacket that was richly decorated with lace, braiding, and oversize buttons. She wore a tiny lace collar and cuffs and high leather boots up to her knees that had turned-down tops. A bright purple sash flashed across her waist just above the handle of a little sword. But she didn't have a cloak (a key element of attire for these fancy supporters of King Charles the First, if you didn't know) and her satin trousers were one leg red and the other blue, which wasn't right at all. It was as if someone had imagined them, but changed some details or simply not remembered the whole outfit quite correctly.

'Greetings, madam,' said Emily in a formal tone of voice that Ezra hadn't heard before. 'We are here to drop off our latest cargo from the Depot. Multiplications of apologies for being late.'

The guard stepped forward slowly in an uncomfortable manner. 'What's your name?' she asked in a low monotone voice.

'Emily.'

There was a pause as she wrote this down very carefully, accentuating each letter, onto a clipboard. 'And what's your cargo?'

'Ahem,' coughed Emily, clearing her throat. 'It's train track for the new desert line, same as last time. It's all we ever bring, remember?'

Another slow, deliberate scribbling of pencil on paper. 'What is the amount?' the guard asked without looking up.

'We've…we've got twenty pieces of track, and…thirty, no forty sleepers,' lied Emily. Ezra could tell from his hiding place that Emily was not a good liar. *What do we do if this doesn't work?* he thought.

More scribbling that took a little longer this time and Ezra pressed his thumbs tightly into his forefingers.

'Okay, go through and drop off the cargo,' the guard

mumbled. 'Once you have disconnected the freight on the siding, reverse the train back out the way you came in. OPEN THE GATE!'

The guard yelled this last part in a way only someone with no enthusiasm or passion can. There was a deep sadness in her voice. It was unmissable and it made Ezra's heart sink to hear it. *The heka*, he thought. *What if it gets me too?*

But before he could worry any further, he heard the sound of the portcullis begin to open. As the massive, iron-bound wooden gate was lifted by chains and pulleys, a series of creaks and groans filled the air, echoing through the stone walls of the castle and making Ezra shiver. Its deep, metallic grating noise was like the growl of a great beast awakening. Ezra gripped tightly onto the train as it shunted forward and began to inch its way slowly into the heart of the castle.

The engine chuffed rhythmically through the entrance and slowed to a halt in the siding. As Emily hopped out and began to uncouple Ezra's freight carriage, she spoke quietly.

'We've got to reverse out of here once we have released you, but we'll wait just further down the track out of sight. There are doors at the front and back of the castle which you should be able to open from the inside. Once you have found the Great Bin Jah Meen and spoken to him, you need to leave by one of the doors and come and find us. We'll take you back to the Depot. Wait 'til we are outside the gate before you get out, okay? They'll certainlymost not be happy with us once they see you so we need to be longer gone.'

There was a clink as the engine uncoupled.

'Good luck, Ezra from Summasetdurivepeck-ham,' whispered Emily. 'And may you find good scones. Remember—we need the fountain to flow again, we need our ibs, or we all run to empty.'

Ezra heard the sound of Emily's feet turning on the gravel followed by the hiss and exhale of the locomotive as its wheels began to turn once more. The portcullis beast growled again as it rattled back down and then there was silence. In the warm, dark green light under the tarpaulin, Ezra closed his eyes and briefly wondered if this were all a dream.

Maybe if I shut my eyes tight enough, he thought, *I'll wake up back in my bed with Parker giving me a warm lick and Mum calling me for a peanut butter sandwich and a glass of milk*. But the sound of scurrying feet approaching on the gravel outside made him open his eyes with a start and, in doing this, his feet accidentally kicked the sheet that covered him.

He froze, hoping no one had seen, but the fact that it went silent again outside meant that Ezra knew he wasn't going to be able to hide anymore.

It's now or never, he thought, so he pushed the tarpaulin aside in one quick movement and, as he tried to stand up, proceeded to catch his shoe on the side of the carriage and fall out in a heap onto the gravel floor. The thud echoed around the castle's inner courtyard, announcing his arrival with a fanfare of sound.

'Er, hello?' Ezra mumbled to no one in particular as he rose to his feet. 'I'd, um, I'd like to talk to the Great Bin Jah Meen, if I may?'

Chapter 13

We'll All Be Red Velvet!

It was at precisely that moment in a castle that belonged to a mysterious magical being, in a courtyard that had been built entirely from an Imagination Depot, in a terracotta town called Ankh Bah, in a world populated by Sahs that was absolutely nowhere at all near Somerset Drive Peckham, all hell broke loose.

The truck was surrounded by eight Sahs, all dressed like the one that was on the gate. Under their ridiculous hats, their faces were filled with fear as each pair of bright blue eyes raised up and up and up from Ezra's feet till they met his face. When he stood at his full height, he towered over them, and his attempt at a smile did not convince anyone that he was friendly.

The Sah nearest to Ezra screamed a high pitch scream that made his ears hurt, and then suddenly stopped which led to a strange moment in which nobody, including him, knew what was going to happen next.

What did happen was the Sah flung his arms in the air and started to run around frantically shouting 'Doom! Doom! It's the end! The end has arrived! Run for your lives!'

And this, dear reader, triggered the other seven Sahs to all simultaneously break into the same state of absolute panic and despair. As Ezra stood perfectly still in the centre of the courtyard, wondering what to do next, the Sahs ran around him waving their little arms in the air and all shouting at once.

'Our cakes have been cooked!' yelped one.

'The end is nigh!' squealed another.

'We'll all be red velvet!' howled a third.

Ezra stood there as a statue whilst all the mayhem moved around him. It was hard for him not to panic too, but, luckily, the little Sahs dashing around in their Cavalier outfits looked rather funny, which put him more at ease. *At least their heka isn't catching*, he thought as he surveyed the courtyard looking for some kind of way in.

In the centre of the space, with Cavaliers running all around it, was a small, raised wooden pool with a water feature. No bigger than a flowerbed, the pool looked very unassuming as water trickled into it through a pipe that would slowly fill a bamboo tube beneath it.

In the middle of the mayhem around him, Ezra was

momentarily transfixed as the bamboo tube filled with water, slowly pivoted and then tipped over, emptying the water inside before flipping back to its original position with a *clack*. The regular intervals between the *clack*s, along with the gentle *gurgle* and flow of water, gave Ezra a strange sense of tranquillity and calm that felt good. *Where have I seen one of these before?* he wondered.

The water in the pool itself sparkled as it reflected the sunlight, but it seemed to have an extra shimmer to it as well, something magical that made it swirl and shine. *The fountain for the ibs*, thought Ezra as a panicking Cavalier almost bumped into him and jogged his memory to keep looking for a way inside the building.

As his gaze reached the far corner of the quad, he found a large wooden door with a giant rusty ring for a handle. Remembering the ibs and the look on Percival's Mum's face as she lay there all curled up, he steeled himself to move forward. He took a first step and just managed to avoid a flailing arm and hat that were running past him.

After a few more steps, Ezra realised that he could dodge out of the way of the Sahs without too much difficulty. And, more importantly, they were all so despairing and full of woe, that none of them seemed to even notice him leaving.

'Great scones, we're all going to be cake mix!' shrieked a squeaky voice as it hurtled past Ezra, dropping its sash and sword. Ezra noticed the slight blade fall to the floor beside him, and in a moment of forethought that even his Dad would have been proud of, he decided to pick it up *just in case* because, well, when you're entering an enemy castle in a new land you never quite know what's going to happen next, do you?

Ezra reached the door, which was about the same size as him, and lifted the rusty ring. It was incredibly heavy as if it were made from solid iron. It felt to Ezra like it was centuries old, not something that had only been imagined into existence a few Thursdays ago, but he tried to remember how different everything was here in Ankh Bah.

He needed both hands to turn it, so he tucked the sword through a loop on his trousers and attempted to twist the handle with all his might. After a few seconds of heavy lifting, there was the sound of a metallic click on the other side and the door inched its way open. Amid all the panicked voices that filled the courtyard—'We'll be flat as pancakes!'—Ezra quietly snuck through the open door and then closed it with a clunk.

Inside, the air was dark and cold, and Ezra shivered as he turned to see the grand, imposing space he now found himself in. It was a hall; a vast, cavernous hall with high, vaulted ceilings adorned with wooden beams and intricate, decorative plasterwork. The massive stone walls on all sides were displaying tapestries, shields and coats of arms with eagles on them. A long wooden feasting table dominated the centre of the room, covered with a rich, deep red and blue cloth and surrounded by sturdy wooden benches.

Chandeliers with flickering candles bathed the room in a warm, dim light, and a huge, intricate stained glass window depicting scenes from chivalric tales cast colourful patterns on the stone floor. The air was filled with the smoky aroma of roaring log fire that sat in a giant hearth to Ezra's left. At the far end of the hall, on a raised dais, imposing and imperious, sat an ornate wooden throne overlooking the rest of the space. But the seat was empty.

Wow, he thought as he took the whole room in. *This place is really cool.* He cast his mind back to his history lessons at school and pictured fiery feasts with flagons of ale, alliances forged and scuppered, brawls and bravado, and history made during the turbulent times of the English Civil War. *This is amazing! Wait, I've got to find the Great Bin Jah Meen*, he remembered. *Where on earth could he be?*

Ezra stepped very carefully over the cobbled stone floor of the great hall. As he moved slowly past the main banquet table, he saw thousands of particles of dust dancing in the coloured beams of light that shone through the stained glass windows. Large knives, pristine metal plates and bejewelled goblets sat on the table in immaculate condition as if they had never been used. He passed the table and the dais with its huge throne before approaching a door on the other side of the hall. It was smaller than the door he used to get in here, but far more ornate. He paused for a moment, taking another deep breath (which he remembered his Mum told him to do before anything scary) and pushed it open.

This was a smaller room, more like a bedroom, or chamber as Ezra remembered they used to call them. There was a large tiger skin rug in the middle of the floor and different trophy animal heads lined up along the walls: an antelope, a zebra, a rhinoceros, a giraffe, and more. A canvas screen standing on wooden poles embroidered with bloody scenes from a battle stretched across the far corner of the room.

In the space behind the screen, there was a strange luminescent deep purple glow lighting up the walls. There were two large wooden chairs sitting either side of another large fireplace with a fire crackling and snapping away inside. Ezra eased the door closed and moved to take a look at the large wooden dresser that was on the wall nearest to him. It was a dark teak with marbled grain that was covered in a lacquer which reflected the dancing pattern of the flames. It had a decorative glass jar of pebbles on top of some silk doilies with a fine spiral pattern that caught Ezra's eye. *They look just like my grandma used to have*, he thought, leaning in for a closer look. As he picked up one of the doilies to examine it and felt its familiar fragility, a voice boomed out from behind the screen.

'Who dares disturb my slumber?!'

Chapter 14

The Very Heart Of A Fire

Ezra froze. His fear at the sound of this voice was interrupted for a split second by the thought *Don't I know that line from somewhere?* before he heard the sound of footsteps on the stone floor coming from the other side of the room. Unsure what to do, he hid behind one of the big fireside chairs.

'Who is there?' said the voice again. 'Who dares to enter my chamber without being invited?'

Ezra pulled his knees up to his chest and wrapped his arms around them tightly.

'Well, announce yourself, vagabond!' said the voice with more force.

'Er…I'm here to talk to the Great Bin Jah Meen,' mumbled Ezra.

'What? Speak up, wretch!'

'Ahem,' Ezra cleared his throat. 'I am here to speak with the Great Bin Jah Meen…please.'

Ezra listened intently to the crackle of the fire and the sound of something shuffling behind the screen as the voice remained silent. He dared to peek around the corner of the chair to where the voice and the shuffling had come from. As he peered carefully, what was a purple glow on the walls behind the screen began to change.

The colour at first deepened, taking on a mysterious and enchanting hue. Then, slowly, as if it were heating up, it warmed to that of an emerging orange that cast an ethereal, fiery glow, painting the surroundings with a sense of magic. Something was happening behind the screen and it was making Ezra feel very uncomfortable indeed.

'And for what purpose, pray tell, do you want an audience with the Great Bin Jah Meen?' continued the voice as the orange grew deeper and brighter.

'I…I need to talk to him about the fountain and the ibs,' replied Ezra.

'He has already told you, *and all Sahs who wish to know*, the fountain will reopen once he has retrieved the stones from the Desert of Apep. Now leave me be, lest you wish to join the Great One's army of Cavaliers?'

Ezra was confused by the language coming from the other side of the room. 'Who are you?' he asked, building up the courage to ask as the orange light took on the colour and shape of flames and started to edge across the walls and ceiling like a sunrise. It was beginning to feel warmer. 'Are you a Sah?'

'A Sah! Ha! How little you know! It is not for me to tell you who I am, you are the one who has invaded my chamber. Identify yourself at once, or you are going to make me angry...'

Ezra tried to edge a little closer to the door because the whole room was now becoming unbearably hot.

'But I just want to talk to him. Can't I meet him? Just for a minute?'

'Are you sure that's what you want, stranger? Nobody else wants to meet him. He's all alone. Especially when someone has made him angry. And you're making him angry right now...'

At that moment, the bright orange luminescence burst and flared into a deep, crimson red that instantly filled the entire room with its heat and intensity. It was as if the very heart of a fire had ignited, casting a burning, scorching red flame that somehow consumed every inch of the chamber. It smothered Ezra in heat and he felt as if he himself were on fire too. He was initially scared at the scalding temperature, but then as he realised that the red had found its way even into the shadow he was hiding in behind the chair, where no normal light should, he felt...angry.

He began to feel cross like he did on his worst days,

when he hated everyone and everything. Like the whole world was against him and everyone was trying to annoy and aggravate and nobody understood. He was cross with the lack of answers he was getting from this frustrating voice. He was cross with this room and the danger he was in. He was cross with the Sahs for bringing him here. He was cross that nothing better was happening to him and that his grandma had died and that no one seemed to care about him and how he was always feeling left out.

And, his brain then working at a super-fast speed, a thought popped into his head and interrupted the anger. He remembered what the Sahs had said. *The heka!* he thought. *This must be the heka! I've got to get out!* and he leapt to his feet, sprinting for the door with only the briefest of glances at what appeared to be a glowing body of burning red light as tall as he was coming out from behind the screen. Grabbing the handle, he ripped it open and fled back into the cold dark air of the great hall.

'Leave me alone! Stay away. This is my castle, my land, you hear me?!' shouted the voice in a tone that made Ezra's insides feel like they had turned to stone and were dropping through nothingness.

He raced as fast as he could away from what he now knew was the Great Bin Jah Meen. *Why wouldn't he tell me?* he thought as he sped through the hall and back out into the courtyard. The Sahs had all fallen asleep, dropped to the floor exhausted by their panic and despair. They were snoring and chuntering quietly with the odd mumbled word whilst Ezra picked his way past them as quietly as someone who is in an almighty hurry could.

He needn't have worried about waking them, dear reader. Despair is a very powerful ib and drains a Sah's energy like no other emotion, even more than anger. These Cavaliers were wiped out by their panic and needed a very good sleep before they would be up and operational again. But our hero Ezra was none the wiser in this regard (how could he be?) which is why he trod so carefully as he navigated his way across the courtyard. He was frantically scanning for another door, and soon spotted one in the far corner. This was a much smaller, less grand opening and Ezra ran toward it. He was sweating profusely but couldn't tell if it was simply due to the sun or if he was still hot from the heka.

He yanked the door handle and squeezed in through the narrow gap to find an empty room. There was no furniture, no decorations, just grey stone in all directions. Ezra rushed toward another door that was at the far end of this room and it opened into another empty room. A further door from this new room revealed another empty space on the other side. Ezra kept running through doors to find room after room with nothing in them at all until eventually he came upon a larger, reinforced door with what appeared to be an inch of daylight underneath creeping through from the other side. He stopped running and examined the exit as he tried to catch his breath.

There was a massive iron key, almost as large as Ezra's hand, sitting inside a keyhole that was set deep within the door. Ezra grabbed it, and with a resounding clunk, it turned with an echoing metallic sound, unlocking a set of heavy bolts that held the thing in place. Once the bolts were drawn back, Ezra pushed at the door but realised it was not yet free to open. A heavy wooden beam rested across the inside and Ezra had to use all his strength to lift it and slide it out of the way, taking a moment before pushing the door once more and watching it slowly open.

As the door swung out into Ankh Bah, a brilliant burst of light flooded the room. Ezra squinted as the cold dark of the rooms he had run through was replaced with a radiance so intense that it seemed to momentarily steal the breath from him. The light washed over Ezra and spilled into the room, casting sharp, elongated shadows on the floor.

As he edged his way out the exit, giving his eyes a moment to adjust, a small face with a big hat and silk ruffled shirt turned to him and squeaked 'What the eccles! Guards! Guards!'

Ezra quickly reached for the sword from his trousers and waved it in front of the Cavalier. This was more than enough to scare the poor fellow, who promptly ran away in horror only to trip and fall straight into the moat.

Ezra didn't hang around to find out if there were any more guards and ran over the bridge opposite the door he had just exited. He then followed the moat all the way around the castle until he reached the train track once more and began to run as fast as he could down the track. He could hear some whispers and gasps coming from the houses that sat near to the tracks, but he didn't have time to worry about those. He was focused on one thing only: finding Emily and Percival and getting as far away as he could from that castle.

It was another minute before Ezra saw the gleaming green engine resting on the track ahead of him.

'Go! Go!' he yelled, waving his arms and throwing the sword in the air to get their attention. 'We need to go! Now!'

The sound of Emily stoking the firebox and Percival releasing the brakes was like music to Ezra's ears as without a cargo truck to climb in, he jumped onto the coal truck and held on for dear life.

Chapter 15

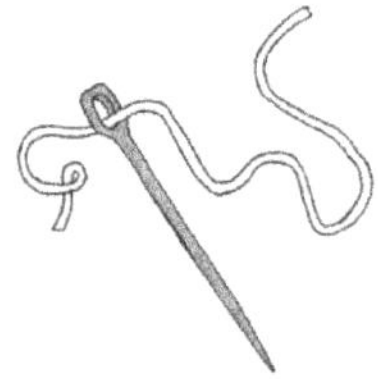

It Can't Be By Accident

The train pulled into the station at Apep and Ezra clambered off the coal, his arms aching from holding on so tight since they left. They had gone full steam ahead on the journey back and no one had talked, their voices drowned out by the whistling of the wind. So, when Emily and Percival jumped out of the cabin, they were eager to ask Ezra what had happened.

'How did it go?' Emily asked.

'Did you get him to agree to put the fountain back on?' asked Percival. He leaned forward with his eyebrows raised. 'Will we be able to get our ibs again?'

Ezra was sitting on the dusty floor and looked down at his hands. He felt awful. He was achy and afraid and exhausted and still a little angry, as if the Great Bin Jah

Meen's heka was still somehow lingering in the background.

'I'm sorry,' he said after a long pause. 'I couldn't get him to talk to me.'

'Oh,' was all Percival and Emily managed to say.

The sun sat high in the sky above them as nobody knew what to do next.

'I tried,' said Ezra, still looking down at his hands. 'He wouldn't talk to me and then...and then I don't know, he got angry he said and, well, it turned the whole room red. It was like his anger was everywhere, and it was reaching into my insides too and changing me and I just had to get out of there.'

More silence.

'He told me never to come back,' Ezra continued. 'He doesn't want to talk to me, I'm afraid. I...I tried to help you. I'm sorry, but I'm not the person for the job.'

Emily and Percival looked at each other and their shoulders dropped.

'I'd like to go home now, please,' said Ezra quietly.

Emily rubbed her whiskers. 'You can't help us?' she said.

'No, I'm sorry, but I can't,' replied Ezra.

'Can't or won't?' interjected Percival, wringing his hat in his paws.

'Can't!' Ezra shot back, feeling that anger again. 'I did

my best, didn't I? I came all the way here through that silly gate thing and tried to help you out! I don't know what else I can do!'

'What about my Mum?' asked Percival pointedly. The anger was spreading to his voice too. 'What do I do about her now? Or don't you persons care about things like that?'

'I do care! But she's not *my* Mum is she? What else can I do? He's too powerful for me. I can't stand up to his magic. I'm not what you think I am. I'm not a…I'm not a hero or anything like that. I'm just a boy…' Ezra's voice tailed off at the end of his sentence, his anger subsiding.

Percival lowered his head and mumbled, 'Fine, take him to the Depot, Emily. I'm going home,' before turning in the dust and walking away.

As the pistons started up again and Emily drove Ezra back to the depot, Ezra's mind was racing at a million miles an hour. When they reached the tiny, oblong concrete building at the end of the tracks, the train slowed to a halt and Emily hopped out.

She opened up a gingham cloth and produced their emergency scone in readiness to put the jam and cream on just the way Percival had done on this most unusual of Thursdays. Ezra watched as Emily used a silver knife to methodically craft a perfect looking scone and then fed it into a small nook that was cut into the concrete structure.

The cake promptly vanished and both Ezra and Emily held their breath as they waited to see what would happen next.

Sure enough, another spinning disc of light began to appear in front of the Imagination Depot. Ezra smiled in relief. As the light began to grow larger, Emily turned to Ezra with a stern expression.

'I know you can help us, Ezra of Summasetdurivepeckham. You might not think you're a hero, but I can tell these things. My heka can read the truth about Sahs, and I think it works with persons too. You are good, Ezra. You certainlymost can help us, you just need to figure out how. We were Sahs without the Great Bin Jah Meen, and we can be Sahs without him again. But you are our key to this, Ezra—can't you see? Why else did we end up in your world? Where you found us? It can't be by accident. Something about all these events—the Shattering, the *Clap*, the arrival of the Great Bin Jah Meen, the spinning gate—has led us to you, Ezra. This story is all connected in some way, don't you think?'

Ezra stood there in silence, not saying a word.

'We will come back for you. It's always Thursday for us, so I suppose that will be the day we'll be here next. I hope that you will reconsider and come back to try and help us again.'

The spinning light had reached its maximum size, its heat and light tremendous, and then started to shrink back down. Ezra, worried that he would not get back through, stepped toward the portal.

'Methinks you are a hero, Ezra the person. You just don't know it yet.'

And with those words from Emily, Ezra jumped back through the closing portal and landed with a soft thump on the grassy garden of 23 Somerset Drive, Peckham, on a wet and boring Thursday.

Chapter 16

Time Is A Strange Thing

Ezra rose to his feet just in time to see the portal close. The next thing he saw was Parker barking and leaping across the lawn toward him. Before he knew it, he was back on the grass and being covered in licks, whacked by a furiously wagging tail, and holding on tight to some warm fur.

'Alright, boy! Alright! It's good to see you too!' said Ezra, meaning it more than he could ever remember doing so before. After Parker had had his fill and sat back looking at Ezra with his trademark quizzical expression, Ezra sat up on the grass and wiped his face off with his sleeve.

I'm going to be in so much trouble, he thought. *I must have been away for hours.* It was still raining so, eager to get out of the wet weather, he walked toward the back door and eased the handle open as quietly as he could, listening carefully for any voices. Hearing only silence, he snuck inside and pulled the door too, being careful not to catch Parker's tail as he bustled through at the same time.

Ezra tiptoed through the living room into the kitchen and looked at the large black and white clock hanging on the wall. He couldn't believe his eyes. It still wasn't even lunchtime. Almost no time at all had passed since he saw the portal appear over the flowerbed.

How could that be? wondered Ezra, feeling very confused indeed. He knew that he struggled with keeping track of time (one of his fast brain books had explained it once by talking about something called a frontal lobe deficit, which made no sense to Ezra), however it was usually when he was trying to be on time for something that it was an issue, not anything like this.

If you, like Ezra, dear reader, are looking for a right answer at this point to this very tricky of questions, I am afraid I don't have one. All I can say is that time passes at different rates all the time, we simply don't pay attention to it. When you're excited it goes quicker, when you're bored it slows down. If you need something to happen it takes much longer than if you don't want it to happen at all. When you miss someone, time slows down whilst they're away, but if you don't like being around someone it feels as though they are always there. If you're a mayfly then a single day feels like a lifetime, but for a giant oak a day is no more than a single breath. It slows down near black holes and speeds up as we get older.

There's no doubt about it, time is a strange thing, and Ezra, faced with his current situation, was in good company as his human brain tried but failed to understand its most challenging of complexities.

Ezra checked the clock to see if it was working properly and it was. Unsure what to do next, he decided to tread lightly upstairs to see if his Mum was still in her bedroom. Sure enough, when he opened the door the same curled up ball remained under the duvet exactly where it was when he left.

'Mum?' he whispered quietly.

No response.

'Mum?' he asked again, a little louder this time.

There was a ruffle of the duvet and his Mum's mess of blonde hair appeared from underneath.

'Hello sweetie,' she replied in a half-awake voice. 'You…you, okay?'

She stuck out an arm and pulled him under the covers. The duvet felt warm and Ezra, who didn't much allow hugs (from people at least), pushed himself up against her back like a baby koala bear.

'What's the matter?' Mum asked, appreciating the closeness but picking up on how unusual it was for Ezra to do something like that. Mums are good at sensing those kinds of things.

'You wouldn't believe me even if I told you,' answered Ezra.

'Try me,' replied Mum.

Ezra's brain was fizzing and trying to come up with ways to tell Mum about what had happened, but it couldn't figure out how to start.

'Is it granny?' Mum asked, breaking the silence. 'I miss her too.'

She twisted her neck to give Ezra a kiss on the head.

'No, it's not…I mean, yes, I do miss her, but that's not what…'

'Come here,' said Mum, turning round and trying to give Ezra a big cuddle which he just about fended off. 'Look, I've got an idea: why don't we bake something? Come on, I know cakes always cheer you up!'

'But…' Ezra interjected. He was trying to somehow find a way to explain what he had done that morning, but as he attempted to formulate the words into a story that would make any sense at all to his Mum, he realised that he couldn't.

She won't believe me, he thought. *I wouldn't believe me either. She'll just get more worried about me and think I'm making it up.* So he decided there and then to not mention his journey to Ankh Bah, or Percival and Emily, or the Great Bin Jah Meen.

Instead, he said: 'Scones. Can we make some scones?'

Chapter 17

A Restless Chimp

The next few days went quickly for Ezra. Starting on Friday, the house became busier and busier as family members and friends came over to help prepare for the funeral that was scheduled for the following Monday. Gramps arrived in Dad's car on Friday morning with an old leather suitcase of his things because he was going to be staying over for a few days.

Usually, Ezra would be excited by this, but since last Thursday nothing was usual any more. Gramps wasn't interested in playing chess or card games or even doing a jigsaw puzzle, as was their usual routine, and Ezra was told off by his Dad for asking. Gramps spent most of his time wandering around the house at Somerset Drive as if he were in a trance, or under some kind of spell, making cups of tea and then leaving them places and forgetting where they were. When he did acknowledge Ezra, it was only for the briefest of smiles before heading back to put the kettle on again or sit in the armchair that looked out into the garden.

Everyone who came to visit Ezra's house was there to help arrange a certain part of the upcoming ceremony, or talk through who to invite and what food to provide, and talk about *logistics* which was a word Ezra didn't really understand. They would talk about the logistics of how to pay for all this, and what would happen with granny's bank accounts, and life insurance, and car insurance, and savings bonds, and pension plans, and so many more things that Ezra had never heard of before.

With the living room and the kitchen full of grown-ups discussing grown up things, Ezra wandered amongst them as if he were in a foreign country, unnoticed most of the time. Whenever they did acknowledge him, he would be ushered out of the room by a friendly face, usually his aunt Marcy or her husband Bill, and asked to go up to his room again to play. Playing was the last thing Ezra felt like doing. *Why doesn't anyone realise that?* he grumbled as he stomped upstairs.

On each occasion, after Ezra had shut his door behind him and looked out of the window, he stared at the flowerbed and thought about the Sahs. What Emily had said to him made him angry.

She couldn't possibly know that I'm a hero. What a stupid

thing to say! he thought, and *Why won't she accept that I already tried to help and just leave me alone?* He was desperate to tell someone about the whole thing, but worried that whoever he told would think it was a dream or another product of his overactive imagination. *How do you know it wasn't?* Ezra's thoughts asked before he dismissed them quickly.

After spending some time adding more glow-in-the-dark paint to a 3D model kit of the moon that he'd been working on, he sat and watched raindrops snake their way down his window pane, imagining a race between two of them, and questioned if maybe there was something—anything—else he could do to help Emily and Percival.

He was cross with Emily for expecting so much of him, but he pictured Percival's Mum bundled up in her bed and felt bad for her. The thought also occurred to him that maybe there was something about the Great Bin Jah Meen which felt like he might need help too, not just the Sahs. *What was it he said? Nobody else wants to meet him. He's all alone.*

When his attention began to wander between things like a restless chimp hopping between branches (that was the way the doctor had explained Ezra's brain to him once), Ezra's mind went to this sentence more than once: *What if that's why he's full of anger and despair? He's just lonely.* But it wasn't very long before his brain moved onto something else and he stopped asking those questions.

On the day of the funeral itself, Ezra was up early as usual and trying hard not to make too much noise. Mornings, before breakfast and his medication, were when his mind was at its busiest, the cheeky chimp hopping from branch to branch at speed.

Before granny died, on a normal summer holiday morning, he would jump out of bed and wake up his Mum and Dad, then race downstairs with whichever one of them had gotten up. They would then watch TV with him for a while until he lost interest and proceed to move through a series of intense but short-lived activities like building a train line with his Brio set, constructing a snow base out of Lego, or inventing a new game out of a set of existing pieces, all the while with Mum or Dad trying to keep up and follow on with Ezra's directions.

They sometimes struggled with this, and it was at times like these when Ezra found his parents frustrating and could lose his temper. He couldn't understand why they didn't just do as he was saying and would interrupt with requests or requirements on what he could use and when he had to tidy something away. It was at these times when his focus on his feelings was at its most challenging and he found himself leaping from one to the other without the time to look.

But on the morning of the funeral, Gramps was

sleeping downstairs on an airbed in the living room so Ezra couldn't even go and watch TV. And Mum and Dad weren't getting up when he went in to wake them, so Ezra climbed out of bed and decided to stay put in his room for a while, building and unbuilding a Lego city over and over again. When he couldn't get it to do what he wanted with the right pieces, he got cross and destroyed the whole thing. At the very moment he had finished tearing his work to pieces, his Mum walked in.

'Ezra,' she said softly, rubbing the sleep from her eyes. 'You need to get dressed now. You're going to stay with Sophie this morning whilst your Dad and I go with Gramps and aunty Marcy to bury Granny, but when we come back there'll be lots of visitors at the house to come and join us in celebrating Granny's life.'

'Can't I come with you this morning? Can't I come to bury Granny? Do I have to stay?'

'It's not really a place for little boys, Ezra,' she replied. 'Besides, I want you to remember Granny how she was before she passed. The fun Granny who loved to play and laugh and joke with you. We can celebrate that this afternoon once the sad part is over, okay?'

Ezra knew this wasn't really a question and when Mum looked at him after she had asked, her face was so full of sadness that it made him want to cry too.

Perhaps, dear reader, people have their own kind of

heka too? And maybe we can't see it, but it's still there working its magic on us whether we want it to or not. As Ezra fought back the tears, he felt so sad that he even allowed half a hug from his Mum, and as she held him there beside her, she started to cry.

'I don't understand it,' said Ezra, his voice breaking. 'Why Granny? What did she do to deserve it? Maybe I could have done something to help her heart? To help her feel happier? If she had a happier heart maybe it wouldn't have given in to the attack? Why do hearts get attacked anyway?'

Ezra's Mum grabbed him by the shoulders and looked at him square in the eyes like she'd never done before. 'Don't you think like that, Ezra Ben Castle. You understand me? It's not your fault. There's nothing anyone could have done. Sometimes these things just happen and there's nothing anyone could have done about it.

'We're all finding this hard, Ezra, and I'm sorry I'm struggling too, but we have to try to be grateful for the time we had with her. If you could have done anything, made any difference to give her even one more day with us, I know you would have. We all would have, but that just isn't how it works. She died with a heart full of love and joy, Ezra, and I don't think you can ask for more than that. You know how she lit up a room whenever she walked in. The only thing wrong with her heart was that it was too old.'

'Will you or Dad get a heart attack?' asked Ezra. 'Will I?'

'No, no,' Mum replied. 'Don't you worry about that now. We're fine.' Mum rubbed her nose on a tissue and reached out to wipe a tear that was forming in Ezra's eye. 'We've got to try to be strong for Gramps, okay? Come on, you get dressed and I'll drop you at Sophie's. We've got each other, and…' her voice cracked as she spoke, 'we've got to try to be thankful for that.'

Chapter 18

He's Not From Here *Is He*

The celebration that afternoon involved lots of different people. Somerset Drive was bustling with grownups of all different ages eating, chatting, drinking, laughing, and crying. Parker was asleep on the sofa having worn himself out with the excitement of having so many different people in their house at the same time. He had frantically chased after each new person as they arrived and jumped up at them with joy, trying to lick them in the face and play, but instead receiving a range of very mixed reactions. It wasn't until Ezra had thrown some bacon bits in the garden and shouted 'Treats!' that Parker had finally left everyone alone. He loved finding treats almost as much as trying to lick people in the face, and after a successful search, he finally retired to the sofa calm, content, and with a full tummy.

Ezra had worn his best white shirt and red bow tie and

spent most of the time sitting on the floor under the table in the corner playing with his football cards. Nobody seemed to pay him much attention if he stayed under there and he preferred it that way. Talking to grownups is difficult at the best of times, and this certainly wasn't one of those. Besides, all the sounds and smells and movement and packed in busyness were too much all at once and felt like a whirlwind to Ezra. The quiet space under the table was a retreat from it all.

The only times he had ventured out were to get some food once the buffet was open, and the time his Mum had asked him to because the testimonials were about to begin. Ezra hadn't heard that word before—*testimonial*—but soon figured out that it meant different people telling stories about things they had done with Granny.

'I remember us riding our bikes to school, pigtails flowing behind us and all the boys eyeing us up once we arrived,' said one old lady with silver curly hair, bright red lipstick, and a big smile.

'We used to go dancing together in the Ritzy,' said a grey old man who had beige cotton trousers, braces, and a walking stick. 'She really had some moves, our lady, she sure did!'

Ezra's ears pricked up when an old lady with a blue beret and green eyes started speaking about her days playing football with Granny.

'Oh, she was a no-nonsense defender, alright! If taking the ball meant taking the man too, she had no qualms about it!' Everyone laughed. 'She loved showing those awful boys what for. And she was always a jolly good sport too, the best winner and loser I ever knew.'

The time arrived for Ezra's Mum to stand up to speak, and a strange quiet settled itself down into the room. Marcy, her sister, was sitting down next to her and had a tight grip of her hand. Ezra fought to focus on what she was about to say because whenever he was nervous his mind would wander more than usual.

'My mother was a beautiful soul,' Mum said slowly. 'Sure, I ran her close a couple of times as a teenager, but she always had the time to talk to me, and always, always was willing to forgive. She was as good at mending an argument as she was those old clothes she wore for years and refused to throw out. Dress your best whether you're off to the bank or the ballroom, she always said. That used to make me laugh,' Mum said, smiling. 'Her love was something special, and I think everyone here felt it in some way or other.' She looked across the room to see a collective nodding of heads. Even Ezra knew exactly what she meant. 'We are going to miss her dearly. She was truly one of a kind, and…' she brought a tissue to her mouth. 'And I am so grateful to have been able to call her Mum.'

With that, Mum sat down and sunk into Marcy's arms.

As the chatter warmed up again, Dad walked over to Ezra and ruffled his hair.

'Chin up, eh son?' he said with glistening eyes. 'Let's get some cake.'

Ezra had gone with Dad to get a slice of the red velvet cake his Mum had made for the celebration, when one of the old couples who were sitting near the dining-cum-buffet table caught his eye.

'And what's your name, young man?' asked the wrinkled old man with skeleton white skin and dark brown eyes.

Ezra didn't much feel like talking, but then Dad gave him a nudge. 'Go on, tell him your name,' he said, faking a smile.

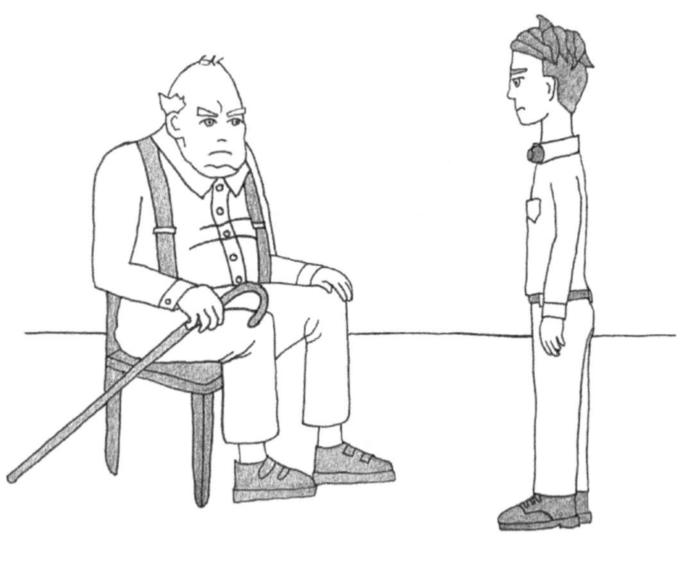

'Er, Ezra,' he replied.

'Ezra, eh? What an interesting name! You're the adopted boy, aren't you? The one from the broken home.' The old man leaned in looking curiously at Ezra. 'Where would you say you are from, exactly?' he asked. 'Your skin's an interesting colour. And that name sounds different too.'

Dad took a hold of Ezra's hand. 'He was born in Southeast London, like the rest of the family,' he replied.

'Yes, yes, but I mean, where is he *really* from? He's not from *here* is he…'

'Yes, *he is*. He's our son,' Dad replied curtly. 'Sorry, but you're going to have to excuse us, we're getting some cake.'

'But not by blood, though, eh?' The old man carried on, not acknowledging Dad's request. 'Awfully good of you to do it—take in a stray like that. Happened during the war, of course, but very generous of you to do it nowadays. Good for you, I say. Give the poor chap a place to live.'

'It's not really like that,' Dad replied, frowning and turning to look down at Ezra who had frozen. Dad handed him a slice of cake and Ezra whipped it out of his hand before walking as fast as he could out the room and upstairs. He could hear his Dad calling after him but everything in his mind was moving so fast he couldn't focus on anything but the feelings that were swirling and mixing and bumping into each other like a hurricane.

He shut the door behind him, dumped the cake on the

floor and began to pace around his room, kicking the Lego blocks and boxes out the way as he passed them. He hated being in his room again, especially because he felt as though he didn't want to be there. He didn't want to be anywhere, and he was thinking, right then, that there wasn't anywhere that wanted him.

Dad knocked on his door and walked in, trying to talk to Ezra again about families not being about genetics and birth, but Ezra didn't want to listen.

'Why am I even here?' he shouted at Dad, fighting back the tears. 'She wasn't really my granny was she? I've never met my granny, just like I've never met my real family, not properly.'

'Don't say those things, Ezra,' said Dad. Caught up in Ezra's emotions, his voice was rising too. 'Please don't do this today. We *are* a family and she was your granny. She loved you.'

'But she wasn't really—she wasn't my real granny, just like…just like you're not my real dad.' Ezra turned away from Dad and kicked some more Lego across the floor, wrapping his arms around his middle after he spoke.

Dad sighed deeply. 'We're all upset today, buddy, so I'm going to pretend you didn't say that because it would be a very hurtful thing to say. I know you don't mean it.'

Ezra turned, anger flowing through him, his whole body tense and throbbing. 'I did say it and I do mean it! I wish I could go back to my birth mum. At least she would understand me.'

Dad sighed. 'We do understand you, Ezra. Better than even you sometimes.'

'No, you don't! She wouldn't make me feel like this.'

Dad took another deep breath. 'I'm going to let you cool off before anyone says any more things they might regret. I need to get back downstairs. You come down when you've calmed down.'

'I'm not coming back down! Not with all those awful people!'

After he left Ezra's room, with the door closed behind him, Dad stood still for a moment in the hallway pinching the bridge of his nose with eyes closed. Sometimes it seems like a badly kept secret, dear reader, but even grownups struggle to control their emotions, and often they don't know what to do with them either.

Dad wiped the tears away from his eyes and then kicked the banister, wincing as he did. He took another deep breath, trying to compose himself, before walking back downstairs and doing his best to pretend that he was okay. Dad had gotten quite good at this recently, so much so that nobody else even knew he was feeling sad. It's important for you to know, as I stitch the threads of this story together, that Dads get sad too sometimes.

After Ezra had calmed down and rearranged his set of

organiser drawers that included all his precious collectables—gemstones, pebbles, foreign coins, magic tricks, model animals, and badges—he heard the sound of the front door opening and closing. Placing his ear against the keyhole, he listened to the guests slowly say goodbye to Mum and Aunty Marcy one after the other, thanking them for the lovely food and offering their condolences once more. When the hustle and bustle of goodbyes finally turned to silence, Ezra slid down to the floor with his back to the door.

After a little while, Mum walked softly up the stairs and knocked on Ezra's door.

'Are you going to come down now, sweetie? Everyone's gone home.'

'No,' replied Ezra quietly.

'Dad told me what happened and I'm sorry you had to hear that. Some people, especially of the older generation, they…they don't always understand all the different ways you can make up a family. And they aren't aware that their words can hurt. He was wrong, Ezra.'

Ezra sat with his knees raised up and his head bowed.

'I wish you'd come out and talk to me,' said Mum, placing her palm on the outside of the closed door.

Ezra stayed quiet. He wasn't sure what was going on, but he felt kind of empty, as if there was nothing good left to feel at all. What he was sure of in that moment was that this feeling was *new*.

Mum leaned into the door and spoke gently. 'We'll be downstairs when you're ready.'

She turned and went back to the living room where she slumped onto the sofa, nestling into Dad's arms with a sigh.

Ezra looked up and stared at the ceiling. The buzzing feelings had gone now and so had his anger, but this new void that had replaced them felt somehow worse. As his eyes fixed on nothing in particular, his mind jumped to a thought out of the nothingness.

Maybe this is what running out of ibs is like. Maybe this is how Percival's Mum feels all the time. And thinking about mums made him remember what his mum had said not so long ago about Granny: *If you could have done anything, made any difference to give her even one more day with us, I know you would have.*

A new idea formed in his mind, and it was so strong in the way it made him feel that it filled the void entirely. With the nothingness disappeared, he grabbed a hold of this thought with all his might and promised himself he would figure out the best way to make it happen. He leapt to his feet.

I've got to do something to try and help Percival's mum so she doesn't die.

I've got to go back to Thursday world.

And that, dear reader, you may well agree (as I've been suggesting all along) is the kind of thing that a hero would say.

Chapter 19

That's A Strange Question For A Wednesday Evening

Tuesday and Wednesday couldn't go by fast enough for Ezra. They were much quieter than the previous days, so the time seemed to drag. It rained almost non-stop and being stuck inside with nothing much to do made the hours go past even slower. Mum and Dad didn't mention what Ezra had said on Monday, and Dad seemed to be trying to pretend that he was okay again. Mum was still in and out a lot, remaining quiet and spending time buried under the duvet, but Dad was having to catch up on work from home. He would be back in the office on Thursday, which suited Ezra just fine because it meant one less person to have to lie to. Gramps was still around but he barely said anything to anyone, so he wasn't going to be a problem.

Once he had decided to try and help the Sahs against

the Great Bin Jah Meen, the decision stuck like superglue, which was pretty unusual for Ezra. He was determined to go back and help out. So much so that he was impatient for Thursday morning to arrive again so that he could get on and do it (which, of course, meant that it felt as though it took forever to arrive). He kept half an eye on the garden, just in case the gate opened on a different day, but he somehow felt as though he knew they could only come back on Thursday, like Emily had suspected.

Also, having something to plan for meant that he didn't ever have nothing to think about and could avoid that empty feeling he had had on Monday, which was good. But trying to plan and decide on what to do next was even more difficult than usual because he was feeling so nervous, which wasn't good.

Ezra was scared to go back, but one thing that helped him feel better about this trip was that he had decided to take Parker with him. With Parker by his side, Ezra always felt braver, and he knew that if he was going to have to try and visit the Great Bin Jah Meen again, Parker would be there to defend him. He wondered if the heka would work on Parker, and thought it would be ideal if it didn't, but suspected that maybe it would because he was always more excited whenever anyone else was, *so maybe the magic might work on dogs too?*

He had dug out an old exercise book that his mum had

given him and decided to record some of his ideas for how to go about saving the Sahs. Organising his ideas was difficult and sometimes it felt to Ezra as if the list was never ending, but by Wednesday afternoon, he'd managed to note down the following suggestions:

1. Try to get into the imagination depot and get it to build a giant cannon (or similar) to knock down the castle and steal the ibs to be put back in the fountain. Problems: this needs me to be able to use the Imagination Depot, and given that the Great BJM had decreed it could only be used for building train track, I'm not sure if this would work.
2. Try the same option as the first time: sneaking in by train and confronting the Great BJM, especially now I know where his chambers are. If I have Parker, I might be able to capture the Great BJM and make him give up the stones. Problems: chances are the Great BJM would be checking the trains now because of last time, so I might not be able to get in that way. Also, Parker might just try to lick him and not help with the stones.
3. Try to build a siege tower like they used in the

old days which would mean I could reach the height of the castle walls, scale them and climb in over the ramparts. Problems: this plan involves having enough wood and tools to build a tower, as well as knowing how to do it properly which is going to potentially be a big problem.

4. Try to build a trojan horse that is big enough to hide me and Emily and Percival. Wheel us in as a present and then burst out at night to confront the Great BJM when he least expects it. Problems: see same ones as option 3. Also, how do we know they would let us in anyway? And what if we got stuck in there?
5. Try to tunnel under the walls like siege engineers used to do. This would involve digging a tunnel underneath the castle walls to gain entry or to undermine the foundations which would cause them to collapse and let us in. Problems: this could take ages, and maybe too long to save Percival's mum. Also, I hate digging. And tunnels.
6. Try knocking on the door and asking nicely? Problem: this probably wouldn't work even if it is what mum and dad always say I should do when I need something from someone else

(especially given the way the Great BJM behaved when I said hello last time).

7. General problems: how do I find the stones? If I need to confront the Great BJM again, how can I do this and avoid his heka? Is that even possible? Thought: where did he come from?

As you can see, dear reader, Ezra had lots of ideas, but no real solutions, and time was running out.

He spent some time on Wednesday afternoon reading up in an old encyclopaedia how to build siege engines and other tactics from the English Civil War that worked in storming a castle (in case you were wondering, tunnelling and undermining were the most effective because the outer walls of the best castles were so thick that they were almost impregnable to other forms of attack) but he got sidetracked on the stories of King Charles the First and Edward Montagu and Thomas Fairfax so he didn't get very far with his research.

Going to bed on Wednesday evening, Mum was tucking Ezra in how he liked it, having read him the latest chapter in his Ancient Egyptian adventure story, and his brain was jumping in all sorts of different directions as he was feeling full of fidgets. Before he even decided to ask one, a question came out.

'How would you storm a castle, mum?'

'What's that, dear?' she replied.

'If you had to storm a castle to capture some precious stones, but there was a mean angry ruler that didn't want you in there, how would you do it?'

'Gosh! That's a strange question for a Wednesday evening, Ezra, even for you!' She smoothed down the front of her jeans and thought for a moment. 'I suppose if I were being smart, I would want to find a bargaining chip and use my powers of diplomacy.'

'Your powers of what?' asked Ezra.

'Diplomacy,' smiled Mum. 'I would find something that this angry ruler wants and then try to strike a deal with him so that I could gain access and get these precious stones.'

'What if he doesn't want anything?' asked Ezra, sitting up on one elbow in bed.

'Oh, everyone wants something, honey, you just have to be clever enough to find out what it is. Now then, I think that's enough seiging-castle-talk for one evening.' She kissed him on the forehead. 'Night nights.'

Ezra lay back down, his thoughts racing once more.

'Oh,' his Mum added as she turned off the light switch. 'And if someone is being that angry and mean, it might be because they're sad about something. Maybe you should consider that too when you're storming the Bastille! Sleep tight.'

I know I've said this before, dear reader, but a good point bears repeating: Mums are pretty useful with this kind of stuff.

Ezra lay awake thinking about his mum's advice before quickly reaching for a pencil and adding another option into his exercise book. He smiled to himself as he re-read it. With the satisfaction of a good idea calming him down, it wasn't long before he was fast asleep and getting some much-needed rest. The valiant quest and true test of his heroism was about to begin…

Chapter 20

A Familiar Flash Of Light

Ezra stood by the backdoor tapping his toes. Dad was working upstairs, which made everything a little more tricky. He was supposed to be in the office but had decided to work from home. Mum was out and Gramps was taking a nap upstairs, and the clock was two minutes away from hitting the time that the steam engine first burst into his garden last week.

He had been jittery all morning and already spent half an hour talking his way through a bowl of porridge that only got half eaten. His Mum's patience was running thin by the time she headed out to the solicitor's office, and it was best for all that she left when she did. Ezra's nerves were getting the better of him and he was dashing around the house singing the same single line from the same song over and over again, which was a bit much for everyone, even Parker.

Once Mum had gone, Ezra watched the car pull out of the driveway and rushed upstairs to pack his rucksack as carefully as he could with everything he needed to make his plan come together. He carefully closed his bedroom door to try to pretend that he was still in there in case his Dad checked, and then slunk down the stairs to the kitchen. This time around, he decided to pack some supplies: a ham sandwich, two bags of sweets, a bar of chocolate, and an apple. There was plenty of room in his giant rucksack that was usually reserved for camping trips, and after zipping it up he reached for Parker's harness and lead.

Parker always thought that getting ready to go out for a walk was a game, and when he saw Ezra approach him with the harness he assumed this time was no different. Running behind the living room sofa and under the kitchen table, it took Ezra a good five minutes to catch Parker so that he could attach his harness and with half an eye on the clock, he got more and more stressed as the time passed.

Eventually, Ezra and Parker were ready to go: Ezra standing by the window, tapping his toes and waiting for the train to reappear, and Parker licking his paws. Ezra kept looking up at the clock and then out of the window every few seconds whilst listening out for any movement from his dad upstairs. A few minutes passed this way and he started to get worried.

What if she doesn't come back? he thought. *What if she*

gave up on me after all?

Another five minutes passed and he was starting to feel really anxious. Parker started whining at the door, wanting to be let out, and Ezra had to keep telling him off. But then, just as he was about to lose hope and head back to his room, a familiar flash of light burst into existence in the garden.

'They came!' squealed Ezra in delight. Parker raised his eyebrows and looked at him curiously. 'Let's go, boy!'

Opening the door and walking toward the white light, Ezra stood waiting by the shed and, after the same hot humming, sparkle, and shimmer as the first time, the gate burst open again and the old steam train shot through, screeching and hissing to a halt.

Leaning out of the window was Emily who looked up at Ezra and tipped her sooty cap.

'Ezra of Summasetdurivepeck-ham, I knew you'd want to come back! Sadly, friend, I must inform you: things have gotten so much worse since we saw you last. We need your help and there's no time to waste!'

Chapter 21

Certainlymost Nothing Good

It took a bit of convincing for Emily to accept that Parker was (a) safe, and (b) the right addition to their trip. Emily was worried about this new type of creature, which she didn't trust one bit, and part of the problem was that initially Parker seemed to feel the same way. Ezra had to pick him up and hold on tight as Parker tried to scramble away from the train carriage.

At one point, Parker broke free and ran round behind the house only for Ezra to chase after him and reappear moments later with the pesky pooch tucked under his arm. After that, Parker seemed to acquiesce and accept his fate. He was docile in Ezra's arms as he climbed into the new freight truck that Emily had attached to the engine.

Ezra wanted to explain that this time he had a plan, but

Emily assured him that he should wait until they got to Apep before he talked them through it.

'A lot has happened since last Thursday, and certainlymost nothing good. You'll see when we get there, Ezra, we should hurry. You can give us the fullness of the plan once we arrive.'

Initially, the train ride felt the same as the first time. The heat and sunlight were immense as they raced through the open expanse of desert at full tilt. It was only when Apep came into view and they started to slow down that Ezra saw anything different. The little town that only yesterday had been made up of a collection of dwellings was almost entirely gone. With a series of mechanical hisses and clanks, the brakes engaged, and, with a final sigh, the train was brought to a halt at a station next to where a village used to be.

Apart from a single solitary tent, the rest of the homes had collapsed. The black, brown, beige, and grey tents lay flat on the ground or in bumpy lumps where furniture stood, their geometric patterns covered in dust and sand.

'What happened?' asked Ezra, aghast.

'Last night there was an earthquake,' replied Emily. 'The whole earth shook. We've had little tremors before but nothing like this. It must be the Great One's heka. He has the power to affect anything, alive or not. I am fearing what has happened to Ankh Bah, Ezra the person. This city could have been torn to pieces in something so powerful.'

Emily hung her head and rubbed those tiny blue eyes. Ezra wasn't sure what to do, but then a thought popped into his brain.

'I have a plan,' he said, trying to sound chipper. 'I mean, a plan to get the Great Bin Jah Meen to return the stones to the fountain again.'

'Well, that certainlymost is good news,' said Emily. 'And we all would love some good news right now. Come with me to see Percival and we can talk through this plan. Whatever it is, I hope that it can be done soon. I don't think we can take any more earthquakes, and Percival's mum, well, my goodness glazes…I don't know if she'll survive this Thursday.'

Ezra glanced at Parker who was currently marking his territory on one of the train station's tree stumps.

'And, please, can we keep this thing out of the tent for now?' Emily continued. 'I don't know whether his dad will be able to handle another strange being turning up unannounced.'

Parker looked over, tilted his head and wagged his tail. His time will come, dear reader, but not just yet…

They all walked over to the remaining standing tent and, after they arrived, Emily paused for a moment outside. 'All the other Sahs of this village are now in here too; there is nowhere else to go. We have tried to tell them about you, Ezra of Summasetdurivepeck-ham, but they were nearlymost dead certain that we were making the whole of the thing up. Maybe Percival might have had a habit of telling some tales in the past. So, please let me go in first and then when they are ready, I will call you in. P.S. and by-the-ways,' Emily said quietly as she started to open the tent door, 'they might not be so keen on you so try to be a bit nice, yes, friend?'

Before Ezra had the chance to answer, Emily disappeared into the tent. He decided to tie Parker's lead to one of the tent poles, hoping that it would hold him. He was not a big dog, but here even he was as tall as the Sahs and so had a decent chance of pulling one of their tents over if he really tried. Ezra looked at him with his sternest look after he had fastened the knot.

'Be good, okay?' he said in his most officious voice. Parker licked him in the face and then started sniffing at the edges of the tent.

A moment later, Emily reappeared.

'It's time to come in,' she said. 'Remember, we need everyone to be calm so just act natural. Heka is catching, so don't start up a problem by getting worried and upset. I'm sure they don't mean it…'

Ezra wanted to ask *mean what?* but didn't get the chance before Emily pushed open the entrance to the tent and ushered him inside. He carefully peered into the cool, dim space inside and saw a collection of little eyes staring up at him in horror. There were ten Sahs gathered across the far edges of the tent in a kind of semi-circle all eagerly staring at Ezra as you might do when you see a strange creature in a zoo. It wasn't long before Ezra realised what Emily meant…

'Oh, great scones!' said one.

'What the eccles is that?' said another. 'It doesn't have any fur and, well, that face is… I feel quite funny just looking at it!'

Another Sah, who looked older and greyer, said, 'I've never seen anything so ugly in my life! I've seen better looking rock cakes!'

Ezra tried to remember Emily's advice, but it was proving to be a little tricky to not take any of it to heart. Emily must have sensed his discomfort, because she hopped into the centre of the semi-circle and stood in front of Ezra.

'This,' she announced, holding her arm out toward him, 'is Ezra the person. He is from Summasetdurivepeck-ham, in a different land to our own, and where he comes from, all persons look a lot like this.'

She waved her hand up and down as she said the last part.

'Well, I shall certainlymost not be taking the train there then,' said the older Sah with a tut.

Emily ignored them and continued. 'Ezra has visited once already and has come back to help us to overthrow the Great Bin Jah Meen, find the ib stones, and restore the fountain to its normal use. And maybe, once all that comes true, maybe it won't be Thursday anymore.'

Emily finished her speech with a big grin that was matched by absolutely no one else in the tent, not even Ezra who was feeling rather nervous, a bit scared, and a lot like he couldn't concentrate.

A silence blew in and out with a gust of wind leaving everyone unsure as to what was going to happen next. Percival decided to step forward and speak.

'Ezra the person, thank you for coming back to help us. I certainlymost don't want to be rude, but whatever you are planning to do to help us, can you do it pretty quickly? My mum is nearlymost gone forever and if we don't get her some ibs soon, well...she won't make it.'

All the Sahs looked over to where Percival's mum was lying, his dad holding her paw tightly in his. There was a lot of shaking of heads.

'And, over there,' continued Percival pointing to a bed in the other corner of the tent, 'is my uncle. Since the earthquake he is now also almost empty too. We can all feel it, the diminishing of our ibs.' Silent nods filled the room and paws took hold of other paws tightly. 'We are all going to be empty soon. One more big disaster and I don't know what will happen to us. Please, we need your help and we need it fast. Emily told us before that you have a plan. Please tell us, what is it?'

'Yes, tell us,' chorused the voices of all the different Sahs standing in front of Ezra and leaning forwards in anticipation (all except the tutting older one who folded his arms and frowned).

Ezra finally moved off his hands and knees to sit cross-legged on the floor. Removing his backpack carefully so as not to hit any of the furniture around him, he placed it down and unzipped the main compartment. Digging around for a moment, he pulled out his exercise book and flicked through to the right page.

'Okay,' he said nervously. His heart was racing and forehead sweaty. 'Before I start, I just have to check one thing. The Imagination Depot: is it possible at all for you to imagine anything other than things to build a train track?'

'Goodness, no!' replied Percival. 'The Great Bin Jah Meen has cast his heka over the depot so that it will only create what he imagines. After the castle was built, he has only imagined train track so it's all we can create. His imagination is so powerful, we can't compete.'

'Hmmm,' said Ezra, picking up his pencil to scribble something out in the exercise book. 'In that case…'

He looked up and across the line of furry expectant faces. *This can work*, he thought, *I'm sure it can*. He cleared his throat. 'Okay then, here's my plan…'

Chapter 22

Her Panic Had Popped

'It'll never work!' said the old Sah standing in the corner with his arms crossed. 'The Great One is too powerful.'

What could be best described as a kerfuffle had broken out, since Ezra had finished relaying his plan. Worry and panic and wonderment were passing through the Sahs like wildfire, each causing the other to get bigger and more consuming. There was also, if you were good at spotting this kind of thing, a little dash of hope and purpose floating around in that tent too, which piqued the wonder and popped a little air out of the panic for some of the Sahs who picked up on it.

In all the hullabaloo that ten Sahs in a tent could make (and it was quite a lot, dear reader, I assure you) Emily stepped forward, took a deep breath, and clenched her tiny little paws.

'Enough!' she shouted at the top of her voice, for her panic had popped and was now replaced with a strong feeling of purpose which she hadn't experienced since the beginning of Thursday morning. 'We need to pull ourselves together! Crumbs! You're acting as though someone's taken all the jam out of your doughnuts!'

Taken aback by Emily's forcefulness, the tent slowed and the heka faded away. Once everything had gone quiet, she continued to speak.

'Ezra the person has presented us with a plan. Yes, it is certainlymost risky, and yes it might not work, but are there any better ideas? Does anyone have a better option than this?'

Ezra took his eyes off the floor to take a look at the Sahs around him. No one was making eye contact with anyone else and there were lots of heavy sighs.

'I think it is an excellent plan,' announced Percival, walking towards Ezra. 'And I think especiallymost seeing as no one else has any other ideas, we should give it a try. I'm ready to do my part. Ezra the person is offering to help us and this is certainlymost very kind. Let's not forget: he has been in the presence of the Great One and he is still able to tell the tale. And what's more, he came back to us again. This means he is stronger than perhaps we know. And better prepared this time, yes?'

Percival rested his paw on Ezra's leg and smiled at him.

Ezra, for the first time since he had been there, felt taller than the tent.

'Yes,' he replied. 'I'm prepared, and with Parker by my side, even if the plan doesn't quite go as we hope, we have our secret weapon in reserve.'

'So,' Emily joined Percival and put her arm around him. 'Are we in agreement? Is that settled?'

Nods spread across the Sahs. 'In that case,' Emily said, turning to Ezra. 'Let's get started!'

'Okay,' said Ezra. 'First job is to introduce you all to Parker. He might look big and scary, but he's really just a big softie, I promise. Let's go meet him.'

Ezra spun around and crawled through the tent door to find Parker lying down with his tongue out panting in the heat. His tail started wagging as soon as he saw Ezra and he leapt to his feet.

'I've got some friends for you to meet. You need to be nice, okay?' said Ezra. He gently ruffled Parker's fur before kneeling down to meet his eyes and pointing a finger at him like Dad did when he was telling Parker off. 'No jumping up, got it?'

Parker looked at him inquiringly, before pawing at his finger thinking he was being asked to perform a trick. *Let's just get it over with,* thought Ezra, taking a tight grip on Parker's harness and steadying himself.

'Okay, you can come out now.'

One by one, the ten Sahs slowly walked out of the tent, eyeballing Parker with great intent.

'Well, at least the beast has fur,' said the older Sah as he stood in front of the hound, inspecting him. Parker proceeded to give him a quick sniff, then a big lick right on the face and the grumpy old Sah couldn't help but chuckle.

'That tickles,' he said, laughing and wiping himself off with his sleeve.

And that, somehow, settled it. The plan, I mean, and the decision to bring Ezra and Parker into their lives for however a brief time, with total acceptance.

Amazing, isn't it, how much one lick from a good-natured dog can achieve? I did tell you he was heroic…

Chapter 23

Chaos And Despair

It took the train a little longer to build up speed once it had set off from the station in Apep. The coal truck had been partly emptied and replaced by six Sahs from the village. Percival's Papa and Mum, as well as his aunty and uncle, remained in the last surviving tent, with his uncle and mum too empty to travel and their partners choosing to stay behind to tend to them. Emily and Percival were driving the train once more with Ezra and Parker back in the freight truck. Parker had his tongue out, lapping up the cool air that began to rush past them once the train had reached full tilt.

Ezra was holding onto his rucksack with both hands and trying desperately to keep running through the plan in his mind, but because he was worried he wasn't able to pay attention to his thoughts, and instead began to focus on anything else that might have made him feel better.

He thought of the time he went to a model railway fair with Gramps and how they saw all the different gauges and mock-ups including one of a train line that ran by the sea. He then thought of the times he went to the seaside with Mum and Dad and how they'd eaten ice cream, dug trenches, and built sandcastles. And that thought brought him back around to castles and the Great Bin Jah Meen and how terrifying the chambers in his giant castle were.

As he shuddered at the feeling of the anger that raised up inside him the last time he was there, he remembered how easy it felt sometimes to get angry. How angry he got with his Dad that time at the beach for not protecting their sandcastle from the toddler who ran into it by mistake. And how angry he had got with his Mum for not letting him buy a model railway kit from the fair. Just as he wondered why he might get so cross with them, Ankh Bah came into view on the horizon, and Ezra got distracted once more.

This time, it looked completely different. The earthquake had destroyed half the city.

The train slowed and entered what was left of Ankh Bah. The previously vibrant and bustling small city had been transformed into a scene of chaos and despair. Most of the terracotta buildings that once proudly lined the streets now lay in ruins, reduced to piles of rubble and debris. The air was thick with dust, giving the surroundings an eerie, otherworldly feel, and making Ezra's eyes sting.

He couldn't see that far, but as they continued through the alien landscape, Ezra caught glimpses of teams of Sahs working together near different wreckage sites, scurrying back and forth and calling out to each other to try and clear bits of broken buildings. They all looked sad and listless and one more disaster away from empty. Ezra's eyes were weeping and he couldn't tell if it was just the dust or if he was crying a tiny bit too.

'We have to stop him,' he said to Parker who had hunkered down in the carriage. 'This plan has to work.'

The train rounded another slow bend and the Great Bin Jah Meen's castle appeared out of the dust as if it were being imagined again for the first time. As Emily pulled on the brakes and the train stopped, Ezra jumped out, tied Parker's lead onto the engine, and found Emily.

'You can see our problem, friend?' Emily said, sadly. 'You can see why we certainlymost can't wait any longer?'

Ezra nodded. 'Okay,' he said, clearing the dust from his throat. 'Are you ready?'

It was Emily's turn to nod this time.

'Okay then, let's do this.'

Chapter 24

No Funny Business, Okay?

The Cavalier guarding the entrance way to the Great Bin Jah Meen's castle was feeling even more despairing now than earlier on Thursday. The earthquake had struck at the heart of the city and it seemed that very little, apart from the castle, remained undamaged. If they had been able to shake the feeling of despair from themselves, they would have done, but it was too deep. Too much for them to simply pull themselves out. It pervaded everything they thought and did, and they didn't see any hope of recovering the Sah that they once were.

It was whilst they were worrying what the Great Bin Jah Meen might do next, that a figure began to appear out of the dust in front of them. At first the Cavalier couldn't work out what it was, but as it got closer it got bigger and bigger and bigger. It was a terrifying monstrosity that was appearing before it. Twice as tall as any Sah, no paws, ears in the wrong place, no tail, and worst of all…no fur!

And then the Cavalier realised that it recognised this figure. And remembered how cold the moat was the last time that they had met. The Cavalier gulped and tried to fight back the panic. He had been told off by the Great Bin Jah Meen after the last time he had met this creature because he had let him get away. He was scared of this furless giant, but he was more scared of the Great One. So as the giant stopped in front of him, he drew his sword and tried to stand firm.

'Halt!' he said. It was the best attempt at authority he could muster. 'Who goes there?!'

Ezra bent down so that his eyes were at the level of the guard and replied. 'I am Ezra of Somerset Drive, Peckham, and I request an audience with the Great Bin Jah Meen!'

'Out of the question!' puffed the guard.

'Please can you tell him that I have something he will want,' replied Ezra.

'And what, bless my baclava, is that?' said the Cavalier, his paws shaking.

'Ib stones that he has never seen. Ibs from another world, far more powerful than those he has taken. With just one of these, the whole fountain would fill with whatever ib he desires.'

The Cavalier didn't know what to say, his urge to panic was becoming too strong.

'Go and tell him,' Ezra pressed on. 'Tell him I'm here and what I bring, and that I want to do a trade with him.'

The Cavalier had frozen, unsure what to do.

'Go on!' said Ezra as forcefully as he could. 'He will want to hear my offer, I assure you. You go in, I'll wait.'

And with that Ezra sat down cross-legged on the bridge, rested his heavy bag on the floor and started to draw patterns in the dust.

The Cavalier paused for a moment, before sighing then retrieving a large key from his cloak and turning to open the door. He walked in backward holding his sword out in front of him and staring at Ezra until the very last minute when he swiftly slammed the door shut.

Ezra had swung his legs over the edge of the bridge and was throwing rocks into the moat when the Cavalier reappeared a few minutes later. The clunk and creak of the door made him jump and he scrambled to his feet as he remembered why he was there.

This better work, he thought.

The Cavalier edged out of the door leaving it open behind him. He cleared his throat.

'Ahem. The Great One will see you now, stranger. But he has told me to say this very clearly,' the Cavalier paused to regain his composure. 'No funny business, okay? Otherwise, there will be trouble of the bigliest kind. Got it?'

Ezra grabbed the straps of his rucksack tight. 'Okay,' he replied before taking a deep breath and beginning his walk into the castle.

He followed behind the Cavalier as he was led through the same dark, empty rooms he had run through just last week (or earlier that day depending on your point of view) until they reached the entrance way to the courtyard. As he closed the door behind him, and followed into the open quad with the fountain in the middle, he paused by a pillar and knelt down to tie his shoelace.

He put his bag down by the pillar so that he could reach his shoe more easily and, if you weren't paying very close attention (which the Cavalier wasn't because he was so worried about getting this stranger to the Great Bin Jah Meen), you wouldn't have noticed his rucksack rustle and slide open. And if you *really* weren't paying attention, you wouldn't have seen, in the shadow of the pillar, a small Sah with bright blue eyes hop out and shimmy away making a wholly unnecessary double thumbs up sign as he did so.

Ezra quickly finished tying his lace and leapt to his feet, chasing after the Cavalier so that he wouldn't suspect anything was awry. He caught up with the guard just as they passed the fountain, and he suddenly remembered where he had seen that design before.

He had done a project at school to try to redesign the outdoor green space, and the teachers had asked the class to come up with ideas for a water feature. Ezra had gone for one like this. It was called a Shishi Odoshi and was invented in Japan. He had liked the idea of them and their history because they were created originally to scare away creatures from farmers' crops. But, also, he just liked the sounds it made as it filled and *gurgled* and *bobbed* and *clacked* on the rock, and the way it kept going back for more, no matter how many times it fell.

'Come on,' beckoned the Cavalier who was now standing by the large ornate door that Ezra recognized as leading to the Great Hall. Ezra ran over to the door and stood towering over the tiny creature in front of him.

'Remember,' squeaked the Cavalier, feeling more scared and despairing by the minute, 'no funny business or…or else.' He nodded at no one in particular and then grabbed the handle and pushed open the heavy wooden door.

After they walked inside, and the door closed with an echoey thunk behind him, Ezra's eyes adjusted to the dark to see a row of Cavalier guards lined up in front of him. They were all standing to attention and trying their very best to not run away. None of them looked at Ezra properly, only stealing the odd glance when they felt sure that he wasn't looking, as he was led past them and through the beautiful hall.

The dust particles continued to dance in the shafts of light that beamed through the stained glass windows and Ezra himself appeared as though he were all different colours when he walked through them. One of the Cavaliers gasped when they saw Ezra bathed in colourful light but quickly slapped their paw over their face to try and keep their composure.

'Did you see?' whispered the Cavalier behind her paw. 'In the red he looked just like…' but she was loudly shushed by the two guards next to her before she could finish.

Ezra was ushered to the ornate door of the Great Bin Jah Meen's chambers and the Cavalier who had led him all that way slowly withdrew into the hall, again without turning his back, with a long slow sigh of relief that was almost immediately replaced by despair once more.

Ezra took one final deep breath, clasped the strap on his rucksack tightly with one hand and then knocked loudly on the door with the other.

'Only one may enter!' came the booming voice from within. Ezra got distracted by that line and was sure he'd heard it before when he was jolted back to the situation once more.

'Enter now, stranger, or you shall regret coming here!'

Ezra grabbed the handle and pushed open the door. This was it, dear reader, the moment to be a hero had arrived.

Chapter 25

I Live Elsewhere

Ezra stepped forward into the chamber. It was exactly as he remembered it, with the same eerie purple glow coming from the far corner of the room. Unsure what to do next, he stood by the door with his foot tapping. He noticed the dresser and the decorative jar and doilies again and it reminded him of his Granny. He felt sad and confused at the same time. *Why are they so similar?* he wondered. *Why are they there?*

Just when he was about to take a step forward to examine them more closely, the voice returned from behind the screen.

'My guard said that you have a proposal for me, stranger. That you have some stones that I may want.'

'Y…yes, that's right,' replied Ezra. He was trying his best to focus on his plan and not the powerful light that was pulsing on the other side of the room.

'Well, explain yourself then. I have not encountered anyone like you here before. You are…different. Where are you from and what are these stones you speak of?'

Ezra pulled the bag off his back and set it down on one of the armchairs in front of him, stretching out his shoulders and biting his lip.

'I'm from my home in Southeast London…I am a powerful outsider too, and I come here bringing treasures from my own land.' He took a breath and then asked before he'd even planned to: 'Where are you from? Where's your home?'

There was a pause in which the sound of the pulsing purple light energy hummed a little louder. After a moment, the Great Bin Jah Meen replied, more quietly than before.

'I don't know where I'm from.'

'What do you mean?' asked Ezra.

'I mean, I don't know where I'm from! I don't know of anything about my past before I turned up here. I have no memories of anything before the Shattering. Here is all I know.'

'So here is your home?'

'Ha! Here is my home! Here where no one wants me and everyone thinks I'm different and is afraid of me! No, here is not my home. I have no home. I live elsewhere.'

'Elsewhere?' Ezra's curiosity was getting the better of

him. His attention was hyper-focused on the voice of the Great Bin Jah Meen. 'What do you mean? Where is that?'

'You ask a lot of questions, stranger. Why should I tell you?'

Ezra put on his brave face and his mum's advice jumped into his head. 'Because I have something you want.'

And because maybe you're sad and I can help.

It was a few seconds before the Great Bin Jah Meen replied, as if he hadn't ever explained this to anyone before.

'Elsewhere is everywhere, and it's also nowhere. My elsewhereness affects every part of me, but I cannot find it when I look for it.'

The purple was gradually gaining a reddish tinge which set Ezra on edge. His brain wanted to start naming the Manchester City 2023 season treble-winning squad, but couldn't because the Great Bin Jah Meen continued.

'When they met me, the Sahs saw me as someone from elsewhere. And they treated me like I was already partly elsewhere, because they thought I might not stay. My elsewhereness sits between us as an invisible wall.

'I remember arriving here in a shower of glass and nothing feeling familiar. Everything felt different. And then the Sahs, they…they looked at me like I was different, and they didn't understand me. They made me feel… They never understood any part of me until *I felt something*. And then they understood that. That was when I discovered my heka, as they call it. The *power* of my emotions. Now when they meet me, they understand what it's like to be elsewhere. To have no home.

'They are finally beginning to understand what it's like to be me. To feel my despair, my anger—can't you see? They finally know what it is to be elsewhere. How unfair it is. Why should it only be me that feels this way? When I fill the fountain with the ib stones I want, they will all know.'

The redness was growing, the walls brightening further and further out from behind the screen, and the room started to feel warmer. Ezra's heart was racing and this sparked his memory about the plan.

'Look,' he said. 'I'm sure you could be here if you wanted to. The Sahs are friendly, they are kind and generous and funny. They would accept you here if you wanted to be with them.'

'I can't keep going elsewhere, and even here is somewhere else. Why wouldn't here just be another somewhere? How is my elsewhereness going to fit in anywhere? You don't understand, stranger. You don't know what it's like.'

The redness began to stretch across the ceiling, its tendrils reaching out for something to grab a hold of.

Ezra's fast-brain was working overtime and he blinked as he realised something. 'But I do understand, I lived elsewhere too, sometimes I feel like…'

'Enough!' interrupted the Great Bin Jah Meen with an explosion of deep red and orange light firing across the floor like lava shooting from a volcano. 'Why are we talking about this, stranger? I will never be accepted here, I'm too different. And that is that. Now show me the stones that you promised, or you too like those sorry Sahs will feel the full force of my heka!'

Ezra, trembling, reached for his bag and fumbled for the zip. He pulled open the main compartment and slid his hand in to carefully retrieve the gemstones that he had packed within. Once he had found them, he pulled them out slowly and held them out in the palm of his hand.

'Here,' said Ezra, holding his breath.

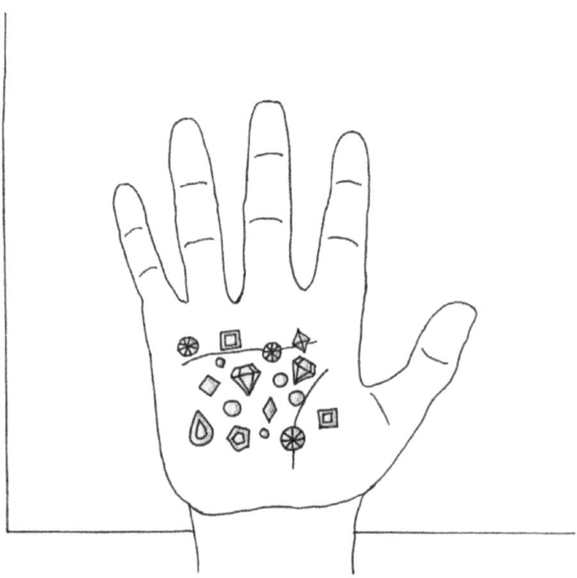

The glow-in-the-dark paint he had used on them that morning was working a treat. Their soft green luminescent light stood out in the twilight of the chamber and shone bright against the deep red colour that all but surrounded Ezra. His prize gem collection, sorted from his organiser draws, and painted to look quite magical in the half light. Ezra waited, hoping that the phosphors in the paint wouldn't wear out at the crucial moment.

'Place them on the dresser, and move back,' came the command from behind the screen.

Ezra obeyed, glad to move away from the red energy that was slowly dissipating once more. He watched intently as a figure emerged from behind the screen and he finally got to see the Great Bin Jah Meen for the first time.

He wasn't a monster. He wasn't a vicious beast or snarling, three-headed hellhound. He was person-shaped, just like Ezra, and about the same size as him too. He had arms and legs and a head and feet. And a face. Ezra squinted as best he could to try to make out the face, but the light that consumed the whole of this person-shaped being's body was too bright and too fuzzy. It had a jagged edge to it, as if it were electric, and it clouded the Great One's features. He approached the dresser and picked up the stones, turning them over in the palm of his hand.

'It's strange,' he said, almost to himself. 'These feel familiar, as if…' he clutched his hand tight around them.

'They have energy, I can feel it,' he carried on, closing his eyes and inhaling deeply. 'They truly are magical. They have their own glow, their own heka, I can see.'

He turned quickly to look at Ezra, as best he could make him out in the dark.

'And you say these can be whatever ib I desire?' he asked. There was an eagerness in his voice Ezra hadn't heard before.

It's working. The plan is working!

'Yes,' Ezra replied quickly, remembering he needed to answer. 'Just place them in the fountain, and you can choose their ib. You simply must wish it as you put it into the pool.'

'Ha!' a flame of red shot out from his arm and splashed across the ceiling. 'Then I have what I want! They will all be elsewhere, as I am! They'll all live in despair and anger like me!'

He picked up the decorative jar full of pebbles that was on the dresser.

'I won't need these old things anymore!' he laughed, opening a drawer in the dresser and tossing the jar inside.

The ib stones! thought Ezra, his eyes widening. *That must be them!* He tried not to look too interested in which drawer they went into as the Great Bin Jah Meen turned to him once more.

'And you…' he said as he began walking slowly toward Ezra. 'You are a fool for handing these over before you made your terms! Did you not know what, like Charles the First himself, all good kings do? Double-crossing and betrayal! These are never far away when so much is at stake! Tell me, what, pray tell, did this stranger want in return for these stones? Not that it matters now!'

Ezra froze. Why hadn't he waited to make the trade before handing over the stones? *Stupid, so stupid,* he said to himself as he stood there, his foot tapping once more. His fast brain rattled through different options but ended up with no alternatives. He was just going to have to ask for them and hope.

'The ib stones. I wanted to trade these gems for those. When I travel back to my world, they will offer me the kind of power that my gems offer you here.'

The Great Bin Jah Meen laughed out loud and flashes of yellow shot out of his body, taming the red for the briefest of moments.

'Those old things! Ha! You can have them, they are worth nothing to me. I was going to destroy them anyway.'

He reached back into the dresser drawer and threw the jar at Ezra. Thinking quickly, Ezra caught it and slid it into his rucksack before anyone had the time to change their mind. *Phew, that was close. Too close.*

With his fist still tightly gripped around the glow-in-the-dark painted gemstones, the Great Bin Jah Meen walked toward Ezra.

'Well, now that we've made the trade, I guess I'll be going,' sputtered Ezra. He picked up his bag and tried to put it on his shoulders as he reached for the door handle.

The Great Bin Jah Meen stepped in front of Ezra, and placed his hand firmly on the door. The red glowed deeper, its energy humming in Ezra's ears and making him feel pangs of the anger he had felt before.

'Did you think it would be that simple, stranger? Did you think I would trust you? When you live elsewhere, trust doesn't come so easily. No. You will come with me to the fountain, and I will do as you instructed with these stones, and we will see if they are as you say they are. If they are not, well…you will make an excellent Cavalier.'

Ezra gulped, his mouth feeling dry.

It was going to have to be Plan B, but whether that would work was, quite frankly, anyone's guess. Heroes don't get it right all the time, after all…

Chapter 26

A Small, Sneaky Sah Named Percival

Now, you're probably wondering what happened to Percival after he snuck out of Ezra's bag not so long ago, aren't you? I know you are the perceptive sort, dear reader, so you didn't miss that not-so-subtle addition to our fast-moving story. Well, allow me the pleasure of getting you up to speed.

Percival snuck out the rucksack and hid in the shadows behind the pillars. He watched Ezra finish tying his shoelace, just as they had planned, and then walk off in the direction of the guard who was leading him toward a large wooden doorway. Percival held his breath as Ezra made his way through and the big door shut behind him. Ezra was inside. It was time for Percival to begin his part of the plan.

He shuffled, half-walking half-crawling, along the edge of the courtyard, trying to stay in the shadows as best he could. Out of the corner of his eye, he saw a group of

Cavaliers slowly exit the door that Ezra had gone into. They were all looking at the floor and not saying anything to each other. Percival stopped behind another pillar and carefully peered around to count how many of them there were.

Ten.

Percival sighed as he realised there were more than yesterday. The Great Bin Jah Meen had obviously brought all his guards inside the gates. This was going to be tougher than he had thought. The ten Sahs began pacing up and down, their oversized boots click-clacking on the cobblestone floor. They looked sad as they stared at nothing in particular.

Percival reached into his pocket and pulled out the things Ezra had given him before they got on the train. He opened up the packet and pulled out the oddly shaped squishy items that Ezra had called 'sweets', before then opening up another strange sleeve of shiny material to reveal some chocolate.

The Sahs had chocolate on some of their cakes but they had never created such a large bar of chocolate on its own. Percival's whiskers twitched as he smelt the rich aroma of the bar whilst he broke it up into little pieces. He was barely able to contain himself and was fighting every urge to eat it, but it was already very soft due to the hot sun, so he knew he had to be strong and get on with his job.

Can sweets and chocolate pull you out of despair, dear

reader? Well, the answer is probably not, or at least not long enough for you to feel significantly better. But could they give you just enough happiness, just enough pleasure—especially if you are a Sah who has a sweet tooth (as they all do)—to make you forget your woes for a split second? Long enough to lose focus on a portcullis gate and miss a small, sneaky Sah named Percival ducking into the gatehouse to pull on the cantilevers and raise the iron beast? Well, he was about to find out…

Percival launched the first of the sweets towards the Cavaliers. This one was a flat white and yellow soft disc that resembled an egg and it flew like a frisbee through the air until it hit one of the guards on the back of the neck. The Cavalier jumped in alarm, spinning around, which caused all the others to jump in unison too and hurriedly reach for their swords.

'Who goes there?!' one squeaked.

'Intruder! Stay where you are!' yelped another as she trembled in her oversize boots.

They all twisted and turned their heads rapidly trying to see where this thing had come from, but with Percival well out of sight, there was nothing there.

One of the Sahs approached the egg-shaped sweet with an abundance of caution. As he reached it, he poked it with his sword then leapt back in case the thing moved. When it didn't, he prodded it again, just to be sure, and then finally leaned down to examine it more closely. As he did so, his whiskers twitched and his nose wiggled. Percival looked on, eyes wide, hoping for the Cavalier to take just one little taste, and, after one more sniff of its sweet nectar the guard couldn't resist. His tiny pink tongue poked out and touched the soft squidgy sugary treat. And then his face was a sight to behold.

'Almighty sponges above!' he cried, before picking up the sweet and taking a bite with an expression of pure delight. 'This is…some kind of magic!'

All the Cavaliers huddled around the sweet, inhaling its perfume. That was Percival's cue and he began launching eggs and chunks of chocolate as close to the group of Cavaliers as he could. Once he'd unleashed as many as he could, satisfied that they were all busy picking them up, he scurried back to the edge of the courtyard and began a slow crawl toward the portcullis.

The Cavaliers, gorging on the sweets and chocolate, their faces ecstatic and blissful as they fleetingly escaped the despair that had entrapped them for so long, worried about nothing else except where to find the next piece of chocolate. They didn't notice as Percival slipped past discreetly and approached the portcullis gatehouse. He smiled to himself as he found the guard's gatehouse open, but his expression soon changed once he examined the inside.

It was full of different levers, pulleys, metal chains, ropes, and cogs. Percival frowned as he tried to work out what to do. After a moment's careful thinking, and with the Cavaliers fast working their way through the sweets and chocolate, he decided to just pull, crank, and twist all of them.

He frantically began pulling on a chain and it kept going and going and going until he heard a clattering and splashing sound from outside the gate. He peered out and the moat bridge was covered in a thick, black oil that was obviously aimed at a potential intruder. He leapt back inside and tugged on a rope. After a few pulls, there was another clunk and Percival looked up to see a little cloud of white feathers floating down towards the ground. Percival twisted a cog over and over and some steel spiked balls started to fall one after the other right on top of the feathers.

It was at this point that Percival let out a loud sigh and suddenly realised that the giggles of pleasure and sounds of scoffing of chocolate and sweets had stopped. He looked back into the courtyard to see, just above ten chocolate covered mouths, ten pairs of eyes all staring at him and the carnage that he had created on the other side of the gate.

There were only two levers left to pull, and as the Cavaliers all began to charge at Percival, with the look of despair and desperation returned to their eyes, he lunged toward one of the levers, yanking it down as hard as he could. The Cavaliers all piled on top of Percival just as he looked up to see a cauldron full of something that smelt a lot like urine tip all over the empty space that sat in front of the still firmly closed portcullis gate. Percival closed his eyes and sighed.

'Stay right there, revolutionary! Your brownie is baked!'

Chapter 27

'Tis But A Definite Tragedy

Ezra pushed open the large wooden door that led back out to the courtyard and, after his eyes adjusted once more to the bright sunlight, a terrible sight greeted him.

Percival was standing by the fountain in the middle of the courtyard, tears in his eyes. He was surrounded all on one side by ten Cavaliers lined up in a semicircle, each one holding their sword out in front of them, pointed directly at their captive.

When he looked up to see Ezra walking towards him, he said in a hurry, 'I'm sorry, Ezra. I tried and I nearlymost succeeded but it was the one lever I didn't—'

'Silence!' bellowed the Great Bin Jah Meen. A flash of red like a firework shot into the sky over their heads, and the earth shook beneath them. Ezra stopped in his tracks just as he had reached the fountain. Everyone went quiet and all that anyone could hear was the soft gurgle, gurgle, gurgle, *clack* of the Shishi Odoshi.

The Great Bin Jah Meen approached the fountain and stopped. Ezra dared to look at him in the light and his colour was more dazzling than ever. A shimmering, static of sanguine scarlet energy consumed his whole body as if he were made of electric molten lava. Ezra felt scared, but somewhere inside for the first time he also felt something new. He felt that underneath that coat of magical armour was a person, maybe even someone like him.

If I could just talk to him, he thought. *Maybe that'll help.*

'So, it seems you did know about the double-cross already, stranger. And there was me thinking that you were not so smart! I should have known better. What is this creature doing here?' enquired the Great Bin Jah Meen.

'I… He was here to try and help me. He's my friend.'

'Friend! Ha! Look at you, stranger. They'll never be friends with you.'

'That's not true, I'm—'

'I don't want to hear it!' interrupted the Great Bin Jah Meen, another flare of red firing up into the air. 'It doesn't matter now anyway. Whatever your plan was, it has failed.'

He opened the palm of his burning hand to reveal the gemstones Ezra had given him earlier.

'It's time for these stones to work their magic,' he continued. 'Once this stone creates despair in my fountain, they'll never want any more friends again. And maybe, after all this double-crossing and betrayal, I should just keep you here anyway as my greatest Cavalier.'

Ezra didn't know what to say as everything grew into a tornado of thoughts and feelings and sights and smells in his mind. He knew that the gemstones wouldn't work, but hadn't figured out what to do when the Great Bin Jah Meen realised this. He couldn't pull apart his thoughts and stood rooted to the spot as the Great Bin Jah Meen stepped toward the fountain pool, closed his eyes, released his grip on the gemstones and tipped them in. They landed with a *plop* in the water and everyone watched the pool, waiting for something to happen.

'Where is the magic, stranger? Why is the water not doing anything?' he asked incredulously.

Ezra didn't know what to say and remained still, his hand in his pockets and his foot tapping.

'Is something supposed to happen? How do I know if their magic has worked?'

The Great Bin Jah Meen flared again and his voice grew louder. 'Why do you not answer, stranger? Answer me, you vile betrayer!'

And suddenly a thought bubbled up to the top of Ezra's mind. *Aladdin. He keeps saying lines from Aladdin, that's where I know them from. He's just copying a bad guy because he doesn't really know how to be one.*

Whilst Ezra was stuck in his thoughts, the Great Bin Jah Meen growled and turned to Percival.

'Bring me the Sah,' he said. The guards poked and prodded Percival over to the fountain. 'Drink!' he commanded, pointing to the pool. 'Let us see if this magic of yours has worked, stranger. Let's see if you really are a diamond in the rough!'

Percival leant down to the pool and scooped up a mouthful of water in his paws before bringing it to his mouth and swallowing it down. He then slowly rose to his feet and everyone leaned forward, watching what he was going to do next.

His shoulders slowly began to slouch as his head dropped, and he started to walk around as he had seen the cavaliers do earlier. He shuffled and moaned, holding his hand up to his brow dramatically and sighing.

'Oh, I'm certainlymost so sad,' he said in a morose voice. ''Tis but a definite tragedy, oh, absolutelymost.'

He continued to wander slowly in circles, edging away from the Cavaliers swords as they watched on enthralled.

'Oh, woe is me!' he lamented. 'This is the deepest despair and melancholy I have ever experienced in my whole sorry existence. I shall never enjoy a good scone agai…' and he suddenly turned on his heels and ran as fast as he could toward the gatehouse.

'Stop him!' yelled the Great Bin Jah Meen, flares

shooting from his arms, but the Cavaliers all stood stock still in surprise and watched as Percival lunged for the one remaining lever. He threw his whole body weight onto it and it lowered with a metallic *clang*.

The portcullis clicked and clanked and groaned before the mechanism whirred into life with a growl, and ten Sahs in frilly shirts and oversize hats watched as the gate slowly raised all the way open and silenced once more.

The fountain gurgled and *clacked* again before the Great Bin Jah Meen let out a riotous roar.

'You think because the gate's open you can escape me! You think you can get away?!'

Ezra kept his eyes fixed on the open gateway, his thoughts clear again.

'We didn't open it for anyone to get out,' he said, his gaze not moving. 'We opened it so that someone could get in.'

The Great Bin Jah Meen turned to watch the same empty piece of air where the gate wasn't. Everyone in the castle courtyard stared expectantly with a collective holding of breath. Ezra's toe tapping on the cobblestones was the only sound to be heard, until…

'Wahoooo!' came a shrieking cheer as a Sah holding on for dear life to the harness of a Miniature Schnauzer came thundering in through the gate. That Sah was called Emily and she was yelping with fearful delight as her steed ploughed his way into the courtyard and stopped suddenly, tumbling her over his head and landing her right in front of the Cavaliers.

Behind Parker, the remaining Sahs from the village, Uncle Leopold and a few more they had managed to pick up along the way, all charged into the courtyard too. When you've got a Miniature Schnauzer on your team, it's not too hard to get new supporters.

The courtyard was suddenly full. Parker was panting, his tongue sticking out, and Emily had risen to her feet, emboldened by her entrance and new companion, and feeling the rush of purpose and adventure.

'Hand over the ib stones and our friends, oh Great Bin Jah Meen, and we shall spare you the hound. Refuse, and you will see what this monster is truly capable of!' she exclaimed.

She was a bit out of breath and coughed after finishing the line that she had been practising in her head for the whole time they had been waiting around the bend of the track. Once they had seen the red fireworks launch into the sky, and felt the ground shake, they weren't sure what exactly was happening, but knew they had to be on their way.

'You think I'm scared of that thing?' said the Great Bin Jah Meen with a little less confidence than usual. 'He will feel the full force of my heka, as will you all, and then he will be my most powerful Cavalier yet!'

'Well, that's what you think!' replied Emily, turning to look at the hound. 'Parker,' she said pointing her finger at the Great Bin Jah Meen. 'Attack!'

Everyone stared at Parker waiting to see what he would do next. He tilted his head to look at Emily.

'Attack!' she repeated, thrusting her arms in the direction of the Great Bin Jah Meen.

This time, Parker opened his mouth wide, licked his lips, yawned, and settled himself down into a comfy seated position on the floor.

The Great Bin Jah Meen began to clap his glowing hands slowly, the sound echoing around inside the courtyard.

'Well done!' he exclaimed. 'A terrifying beast indeed!'

'Ezra!' shouted Emily. 'Do something!'

And with that, Ezra's super-fast brain rattled through all sorts of possibilities and, this time, came up with exactly the thing to do. He reached into his rucksack, pulled out the squashed ham sandwich he had brought with him, and yelled 'Parker—treats!' before hurling it right in the middle of the Cavaliers.

Parker's nose twitched, his ears pricked up, and within a split second, he was off.

Perhaps you can guess what happened next, dear reader?

Well, you're right. As Parker the giant dog bounded toward them with a glint in his eye only the sound of 'treats!' can give, the Cavaliers panicked like they've never done before.

'It's all over this time!' howled one.

'This really is the end of my bake!' cried another.

'We're all for the cake mixer now!' screeched another guard, tripping over their boots.

And they all began to run around like headless chickens, waving their arms and squeaking in fear. Once Parker had found the sandwich and gobbled it down in one delicious mouthful, he thought this game the Cavaliers were playing looked great. He started chasing after them, barking, and jumping up, loving the excitement and energy of it all. He was catching *their* heka it seemed. As you can imagine, it was absolute bedlam inside the castle courtyard, but the one place where time felt as though it was standing still was in the space between Ezra and the Great Bin Jah Meen.

'You have betrayed me for the last time,' growled the Great Bin Jah Meen. The energy around his body was growing even stronger and louder. 'Now you will feel what it truly is to be angry, and you too will punish your friends because of it.'

'We were here to help,' rushed Ezra as Parker dashed past, knocking over one of the Cavaliers and licking him in the face.

Even though Ezra didn't spot it, some of the Sahs from Apep did because, well, it took them by surprise when the Cavalier started laughing. Bowled over as he was, lying on his back with Parker leaning over and licking him, the Cavalier was giggling uncontrollably and something began to change. You could see his body relax as he lost control and gave in to the laughter. Parker's heka was catching too. And, all of a sudden, as Parker bounded off to find another Cavalier to lick, he sat bolt upright and looked down at his clothes, wondering what on earth he was wearing.

'You're not here to help, stranger,' shouted the Great Bin Jah Meen. 'No one ever helps me! And now you'll know what that's like!'

'We are here to help! I know you're not really a bad guy. You stole all your lines from Jafar! You're just sad about being elsewhere, and that's okay. You just need to—'

'No, I'm not! You're making me annoyed! You just need to stop!'

As he said these last words, there was an explosion of red and the whole courtyard became bathed in the colour. Ezra could see the anger instantly appear in all the expressions of the scarlet Sahs around him. And he could feel his own anger growing too. He was angry at Percival for failing to open the gate earlier. He was angry at himself for not carrying out the plan as he had hoped. He was angry at Parker for being too soft to get them out of there. He was angry at the thought that maybe all his anger had made people feel like this too.

'This is all his fault!' sniped the Great Bin Jah Meen, pointing at Ezra. 'He brought you here with his strange ideas and look where he got you: under my heka! He's the one who has ruined your lives! Attack *him*!'

The Great Bin Jah Meen's voice was angry and sad and wobbly and powerful and confused, but it worked because all the Sahs who had come into the courtyard looked over at Ezra with a hateful despair. Their eyes glowered at him in the shade of the red light that covered them all. The heka was working and they had no power to stop it. They started walking toward Ezra with faces that looked like thunder, and intent in their eyes. Ezra tried to run away but tripped on the Shishi Odoshi and fell, hitting the cobblestones hard. He turned over just in time to see Percival and Emily leap onto his chest and pin him down.

'I was trying to help!' screamed Ezra. He desperately tried to wriggle free, but his words couldn't be heard over the throbbing hum of anger that was everywhere. And all of these Sahs piling on top of him, and the sense of feeling trapped as he pushed and squirmed and felt more and more out of control, reminded him that he felt angry too. Really angry.

They think this was my fault? I came here to try and save them, why don't they see? It's all their fault for making me come here! They couldn't save themselves, why did I bother trying to save them? And now we've failed and I'll never leave…

Just as his anger was beginning to turn to despair and he thought of his parents and how angry he was with them for not helping him, but also how sad he was that he might never see them again, he saw the tremendous sight of Parker leaping clean over his head, and the heads of all the Sahs that were on top of him.

The Great Bin Jah Meen was, at this point, a glowing ball of light, showering his heka like a volcano, but Ezra's brain moved so fast that it somehow escaped the anger for one moment and watched as Parker carried on and jumped once more into the air. As if he were in slow motion, Parker glided through the air in a fateful bound before landing and clattering right into the Great Bin Jah Meen, knocking him over. Parker was lost momentarily in the glowing red light and Ezra, being drawn back into the heka, was furious with him for doing such a reckless thing. As his anger grew and grew to a point where he almost shouted at himself, a strange sound came from the volcanic ball of light.

It wasn't easy to hear to begin with because of the humming of the energy, and the anger that filled Ezra's ears, but as the loud throbbing hum began to quieten a little, and the ball of light began to shrink, Ezra's senses started to separate again, and he could hear the unmistakable sound of…

Laughter.

Chapter 28

The Jelly Bit Of A Jaffa Cake

It started as a little giggle, turned into a light chuckle, briefly became a throaty chortle, and then finally burst into full blown guffaws.

The Great Bin Jah Meen was rolling around on the floor and laughing uncontrollably under the weight of Parker who had his front paws on his chest and was trying with great persistence and determination to lick the big warm face that was right in front of him.

'Get off!' yelped the Great Bin Jah Meen with words that he could barely get out through his giggles.

But as Parker continued, enjoying the tussle as if it were a game, the ball of red light that surrounded the two of them began to shrink. In between trying to palm off persistent Percival and the other Sahs who were wrestling to grab hold of his arms, legs and ears, Ezra caught glimpses of this shrinking ball and saw it get smaller and smaller. The laughter carried on and Parker's tail wagged more and more, and the light got less and less until suddenly it didn't cover the courtyard anymore.

Percival and Emily stopped their grappling, sat up, taking their hands off Ezra, and stared with all the other Sahs at the incredible sight of the Great Bin Jah Meen turning from dark red, to deep purple to a new colour they had never seen: a light orange. The colour of orange juice and warm sunshine and the jelly bit of a Jaffa cake.

Parker had finally had his fill, and after nuzzling his nose into the Great Bin Jah Meen's neck and giving him one final lick, he bounded off to hunt for any more treats that might have been left lying around.

Ezra, the Sahs and the Cavaliers all slowly stood to their feet glancing at each other and then looking back over at the Great One who was lying with his back on the cobblestones staring up at the sky. The intense orange radiance that surrounded him began to cool slightly, resembling the warm glow of a setting sun on a summer evening. The colour appeared to dance across his body, casting a vivid brilliance that started to soften into a more subdued shade. As if the sunlight of his body were merging with lush greenery, the once fiery orange began to relinquish its dominance, making way for the emergence of a deep green.

It's hard to describe what it looked like, dear reader, but try to picture the transformation as a subtle play of shadows and highlights, as if the colours were engaged in a graceful dance. The deep green, reminiscent of a great pine forest, gradually infiltrated his body, imbuing the courtyard with a sense of tranquillity and renewal that everyone could feel. For the tiniest of moments, everyone felt peaceful in a way they couldn't describe. Everything just felt *okay*.

And then with a blinding flash of rainbow light and a sound like a hurricane in reverse, the green was gone. Ezra covered his eyes to protect them, but when he opened them again, there, sitting in the middle of the courtyard, next to a Shishi Odoshi fountain, was a boy. A boy who was sitting up and climbing to his feet.

A boy who looked terrified.

A boy who burst into tears.

'Where am I?' he asked, crying into his hands. 'I want to go home.'

Chapter 29

Find Your Own Somewhere

Ezra stepped toward the boy, who still had a wide berth from everyone else. His sense of purpose was gleaming and something felt *right* about talking to this boy. He felt hyper-focused and alert.

I can help him, he thought, like all good heroes do.

'I thought you said you had no home?' Ezra asked, trying to examine the boy whose face was hidden behind his hands as he cried.

He looks weirdly familiar, thought Ezra as he took another step.

'Did I? I…I don't remember. I was feeling so… Where am I? There was a shatter of glass and I was here. How did I get here?' A gust of wind blew through the castle courtyard. 'I want to go home,' he pleaded again in between sobs.

Ezra took another step. 'You're in Ankh Bah, in a castle you created. You said you were elsewhere, do you remember that?'

'I…' the boy sniffed and began to rub his eyes. 'That's just how I feel sometimes. Sometimes it gets too much and…well, I don't feel like I belong anywhere.'

Ezra moved forward once more and was now standing next to the fountain. He was almost close enough to touch the boy. They were the same height and build, and without the powerful light and aura around him, he didn't seem scary to Ezra at all.

The Shishi Odoshi went gurgle gurgle gurgle *clack.*

'You know,' said Ezra. 'Sometimes I feel like I'm elsewhere too.' His mind was racing and what he'd been trying to say earlier all came out at once.

'Some of the kids in my class, usually when I talk too much or can't keep up with what they're saying, treat me like I'm elsewhere even when I'm right there. My birth mum and birth dad, well, they must think I'm elsewhere because they aren't here to know where I am. I got placed elsewhere because they couldn't look after me, which meant I really was *literally* elsewhere for a while, which I still don't really understand. It also kind of means that I don't really know where I'm from so I guess I'm from elsewhere too, if you think about it.

'And that's not even the half of it. When I get cross,

school puts me elsewhere so that I'm away from everyone else. And sometimes I sort of end up putting myself elsewhere unintentionally by getting so cross that people don't want to be near me.

'And when I'm with my family, because I look different, some people treat me as though I'm elsewhere too, and that really makes me angry. And when I'm angry, when I'm right in the middle of it, it feels good. It feels powerful. It feels *right*. It's only when I stop that I realise—'

'That it didn't help anything and only made you feel more like you were elsewhere?' interrupted the boy with surprise in his voice.

'Yes…that's what I was going to say,' Ezra said, taken aback. 'But, you know,' he continued, looking up at the sky, 'I don't feel like that all the time. And I think I forget that when I'm feeling all jumbled and whipped up and can't remember on my own. So even if you feel like you're elsewhere, with a bit of help you can always find your own somewhere. And maybe it's hard to appreciate that sometimes, and maybe you'll make mistakes and get things wrong again, and say unkind things and feel bad about it, but home is…'

'Home is where people will love you and try to understand you anyway,' continued the boy, the clouds clearing from his voice. 'And home is where you can try to…'

'Learn to feel...*loved*.' Ezra finished with a smile, and the boy smiled too, taking his hands away from his face and looking at Ezra for the first time.

'I'm trying to be better at that...' Ezra replied but stopped speaking when he saw the boy's face.

He was astounded. Bemused. Totally befuddled.

The boy looked exactly like him. They both frowned in precisely the same way and tipped their heads to the side to look more closely.

'How can it...' trailed off Ezra as his mind went faster than a rollercoaster.

'That's funny,' said the boy quizzically, 'you look just like me.'

'I think you mean you look just like *me*,' Ezra replied.

'My name is Benjamin, by the way. What's yours?' asked the boy, reaching out to shake Ezra's hand.

'I'm Ezra…wait, you're called Benjamin?'

'Yes, I think I am... *Something* Benjamin anyway,' he said, frowning. 'I can't remember the rest. Maybe there's more, I'm not sure. Wha… Woah! Something weird is happening,' exclaimed Benjamin the boy as he was about to take Ezra's hand and looked down at his arm. It was flickering in and out of existence, as if there were a light switch somewhere turning it off and on, but with less power each time it came back. Ezra stepped back as the rest of Benjamin's body began to do this too, gradually flickering out and becoming less visible each time.

'I think I'm…I'm going somewhere,' he said with a look of astonishment on his disappearing face. 'I can feel it. It's like…*magic*. It feels good, like I'm a piece of something that finally got found. Maybe I don't have to be elsewhere, maybe I have a place of my own. Wait, it feels like I'm going ho…'

And, in a brilliant burst of bright rainbow light, he disappeared.

Chapter 30

Time To Go Home

Ezra frantically looked around to see where Benjamin had gone, but he couldn't see him anywhere. He had so many questions he wanted to ask but was still reeling from the brilliant burst of light that had somehow touched his insides. It felt strangely familiar. And then he remembered where he had seen it before.

He came in a shower of glass, and had no memory of anything before that, he thought. Ezra cast his mind back to that argument on the first day of summer, and pictured his reflection on the glass as it flew to the floor. *I was so angry…I made a wish, did it somehow in a strange way…come true? The glass in the bakery was the same. The Shattering, did I do that? Maybe he was a piece of…me? Is that even possible? 'Something Benjamin' he said his name was, same as me. That can't be right, can it?* he thought, his feelings all over the place.

'What the eccles happened?' asked Emily, appearing next to Ezra and examining the ground where Benjamin had stood. 'Did he…did he just do a vanishing?'

'Yes, I think so,' replied Ezra. 'I hope so. I feel like he's been found.' He turned to Emily. 'You know,' he added, 'he said his name was Benjamin. *Something* Benjamin.'

'Yes, exactly,' replied Percival, popping up next to Emily and tutting. 'As we certainlymost informed you, on many occasions: *Bin Jah Meen*. Do your ears need de-fluffing, Ezra the person?'

'My middle name is Benjamin,' he said, almost to himself. 'I'm a *Something* Benjamin too. Ezra *Benjamin* Castle.'

'And my middle name is Ernest,' replied Percival. 'What's the big deal?! We've saved the city! We can restore the ibs to the fountain! We don't all have to be miserable in the smelly pits of despair. This is the goodest of good news!'

And Emily and Percival and all the other Sahs started to whoop and holler and cheer as they danced about the courtyard. But it didn't last long before they looked exhausted.

'Ibs,' mumbled Emily looking at Ezra. 'We need the ibs.'

Ezra hurriedly fished out the jar of pebbles from his bag

and took one last careful look at them before removing the lid and tipping them back into the fountain. As they plopped in one after the other, a beautiful light display of all the colours of the rainbow burst into life on the surface of the water, and the Sahs all reached down to drink some, looking immediately refreshed as they did. Percival wiped the water off his whiskers with a wide grin on his face, before scooping up some into a container and hanging it around his neck.

'Time to go home, Ezra of Summasetdurivepeck-ham,' he said. 'I've got a mum who needs my help.'

So do I, thought Ezra.

They all left the castle through the open portcullis gate and climbed back on the train to Apep. The Cavaliers returned to find their families, grateful to have drunk from the fountain and to be finally free from their despair. The Sahs who had joined the charge that day from Ankh Bah, including Uncle Leopold, drank their fill and then ran joyfully out to spread the news across the city that the Great Bin Jah Meen was in control no longer.

As the train containing Ezra, Parker, and the Sahs pulled into Apep once more, Percival rushed off to deliver the fountain water to his mum and uncle but not before thanking Ezra profusely for all his help with a grin and a very forceful handshake. The other Sahs from the village all lined up to do the same, each one shaking his hand and then, recognising that heroes come in many forms, giving Parker a tickle under the ear much to his delight.

Once Percival and the other Sahs had left, Emily turned to Ezra.

'Is it time to go home, Ezra the person?' she asked.

'Yes, I think so,' he replied.

'Good job I came prepared then,' Emily smiled, showing Ezra a gingham tablecloth with all the ingredients for a delicious scone inside. 'Come on, its nearlymost time for you to get going.' she added, climbing back into the steam train for Ezra's final journey to the Imagination Depot.

As they rode slowly along the track with Parker's ears flapping in the wind once more, Ezra began to wonder what the Sahs would do next.

'Now that the Imagination Depot is going to be working again,' he said, 'you can rebuild your village and city?'

'Yes, absolutelymost. It will be a big job, but we will work together to get it done,' she replied, leaning out of the cabin window.

'What will you build this time?' Ezra wondered. 'If it will build anything you can imagine, the possibilities must be endless.'

'We will rebuild our village and city exactly as they were,' replied Emily.

'If you can build anything in the imagination depot, why not create something brand new?' Ezra asked, incredulous. 'Why not build a city in the sky or a golden tower or an underwater kingdom or…well, anything! Why rebuild the city as it was?'

'Because this is our home, Ezra the person. This is where we live. It's how we want things to be.'

Ezra pondered that thought for a moment until he got distracted by the sight of the oblong box appearing at the end of the line.

Emily slowed the train to a halt, stepped out and began preparing the scone. Just as she was about to place it in the nook, Ezra had a flash of inspiration.

'Wait, if the depot works again, can I give it a go? Can I imagine something before I go?' he asked.

Emily smiled. 'I don't see why not. Just not anything so big we'll have to tidy it up, please!'

Ezra laughed. 'Don't worry, it's going to be small, I promise. How does it work?'

Emily pointed at the nook. 'You place your hand in here and imagine the thing you want. Just think of one thing otherwise it gets confused. Once it has picked up your imaginings, if it's small, it will appear by the front. If it's big, the portal door will open and you'll have to go in and get it.'

'Okay,' said Ezra walking up to the concrete shape and taking a deep breath. 'Here goes!'

He closed his eyes tightly and pictured with his best concentration the object that he wanted to create, before slowly placing his hand in the nook. He felt something inside his mind, a movement as if there were something in there having a nose around searching for something before it suddenly stopped and a *bing!* sounded out from the depot.

Ezra slowly opened his eyes and there, floating in the air in front of the depot, was a plate with a still hot, cheesy, doughy, and delicious barbecue chicken pizza.

'What the eccles is that?!' asked Emily, peering at the pizza as if it were an object from outer space. Parker's nose twitched.

'Pizza!' announced Ezra with great pride. 'You guys only eat cakes, right?'

'Yes, but…'

'Well, then allow me to introduce you to something that will blow your mind! I think if you like cake you're going to love pizza! Consider it my parting gift to you. Go on, take a bite!'

Ezra grabbed the pizza and ripped off a slice to give to Emily. She looked at it and gave it a sniff before taking a tiny bite. As she chewed, her frown gradually turned into a smile of pure delight.

'Wow!' she said, taking an enormous bite. 'This is amazing!'

'You're welcome!' said Ezra. He felt very pleased with

himself as he took a bite of his imagined pizza too. It tasted just as he had pictured.

Emily and Ezra sat on the sand and polished off the pizza in no time. Parker was more than happy to help out too. Once they had finished, and Emily had licked her whiskers and paws, she walked up to Ezra and gave him a big, big hug.

'Thank you,' she said as she held him tight. 'For everything.'

Ezra hugged her and her warm, soft fur and it felt good. Emily let go and reached for the scone that was sitting on the tea towel beside her.

'Okay, let's get this gate open. I hope the scone thing still works,' she said to herself with a frown. 'Hmmm, I'll add a dollop of imagination this time too, just in case.'

Emily placed the scone in the nook and closed her eyes. When she opened them, there was a smile on her face as she stepped back and watched a vortex of spinning bright white light appear in front of the depot once more. Ezra smiled too as the warm humming light grew to its full size in front of them.

She drove the train through and brought it to a halt once more. Ezra and Parker climbed out of the coal truck and stood facing Emily on the grass.

'I told you you'd come back,' Emily smiled. 'And now

we know persons have heka too, it's certainlymost good to remember where you are in case we get into another pickle.'

'Persons have heka too?' Ezra asked.

'Oh yes,' smiled Emily. 'How else do you think you and Parker defeated the Great Bin Jah Meen? The only heka more powerful than anger is love. And yours and Parker's was simplymost too deep and too infectious to be ignored. You're more powerful than you realise.'

She grabbed the whistle chain and let out a loud *peep peep* before releasing the brakes.

'You might see us again, my friend. And maybe not even on a Thursday, huzzah! Our stories are connected somehow, you see? I told you so! Now, Ezra the hero,' she continued, 'go be *somewhere*!'

Chapter 31

A Finished Cup of Tea

Ezra raced into the house through the backdoor and checked the time. A mere ten minutes had passed since he left. The difference this time though was that Ezra wasn't surprised to find out. As he closed the backdoor behind him and walked into the kitchen, his Dad was standing there making coffee.

'Hey, buddy,' he said, not looking up. 'You been out in the garden?'

Ezra paused before replying, 'Sort of.' He was still trying to find the right words to say what he wanted to say.

Just then, he heard the sound of the front door open and close, and the jingle jangle of keys in the key pot. Ezra's Mum slowly appeared in the kitchen doorway with her shoulders hunched, tired eyes, messy hair and a pale face.

She's running on empty, thought Ezra. Maybe humans

need to restore and replenish their ibs too, dear reader, only they don't have stones and a fountain to do it for them.

Seeing his mum like that, after all the drama and stress and excitement of his journey that morning, was too much for him to bear. He dropped his rucksack, ran over and, almost knocking her down, gave her a big bear hug.

'Hey, hey, what's this all about?' she said, taken aback.

'I'm sorry. I…I think maybe I thought I was elsewhere and maybe I do sometimes feel that way but I'm also somewhere and I know you are too, and—'

'Slow down! What do you mean elsewhere?' said mum trying to keep up.

'As in not really here, but I do have my own somewhere and I'm trying to get better at remembering that. And I'm sorry for…for not realising that people get empty too sometimes.'

And, as he hugged his mum and his Mum hugged him back, Ezra burst into tears. As if a tap had been turned on, the tears flowed and he started to sob uncontrollably for the first time since the news on that fateful Thursday afternoon.

'It's okay, sweetie. It's okay, I'm here,' said his mum, holding him tightly. Ezra's dad put down his coffee and joined in the hug. Ezra, the jam in the parent sandwich, finally allowed himself to give into a hug in a way he had never done before.

I'm here too, he thought. *I'm somewhere.*

As his tears began to dry, he looked up at Mum and Dad and saw that they were crying too. And they weren't only holding him, but also each other. They saw him look up and smiled with a lightness in their face that looked like orange juice or warm sunshine or the jelly bit of a Jaffa cake.

And then the kitchen door swung into Mum and they all nearly fell over.

'What's all this?' Gramps asked, barging his way in and rubbing some sleep out of his eyes.

'Just a family cuddle, Dad,' said Mum with a smile on her face as she fetched a tissue from her pocket.

'I see,' he replied, shuffling past, still not quite woken up yet. 'What was that commotion in the garden just now? Darned thing woke me up.'

'Probably just a fox, Gramps,' said Dad, absent-mindedly turning back to his coffee. 'Or noise from that building site over the back. Ezra was out there not so long ago, might have been him. Never you mind.'

'Hmph,' said Gramps. He shuffled over to the sink and put a finished cup of tea inside. 'Sounded like there was some kind of contraption out there to me.'

Ezra's eyes widened and he looked down at Parker who tilted his head to one side and, with the gentlest of movements, Ezra could have sworn he winked.

Mum rubbed Gramps' hand and placed a kiss on his cheek. 'Well at least you finally finished a cup of tea! Seeing as we are all here, why don't we play a board game, eh?'

And Ezra saw the hope in his mum's face and heard the purpose in her voice, and he grinned a grin as big as a Sah eating pizza for the very first time.

Chapter 32

True Heroes Are Everywhere

And that, dear reader, is the end of our tale—all but one final, conspicuous, delightful detail—concerning the salubrious Sahs of Ankh Bah. Legend has it that a strange and mighty downpour struck the city not long after Ezra the Person had left. It rained and it poured like never before as if the heavens themselves were bereft. After the much talked about Shattering and *Clap*, came the great and almighty Shower, another awesome display of my realm of stories' magical power.

And do you know what happened after that momentous, torrential rain had stopped? Well, as everyone peered out their open windows, the sun seemed to have hopped. It moved just a little further across the sky, and as Emily, Percival and all wondered why, the stories walked away from what would soon become the most welcome

Friday ever.

So, perhaps you know our hero Ezra a little better now? And maybe your opinions of him have changed somehow?

I hope you understand why I said he was a remarkable find? And the power of us stories for your story-shaped minds?

You see, true heroes don't run around getting everything right all the time. True heroes get things wrong but then look for other answers to find. True heroes make mistakes and feel lonely sometimes. True heroes can get angry, feel cross and lose their mind.

But true heroes also care for others, and build relationships, and are brave enough to take that first step toward trust. True heroes love, and learn to love, and learn to *feel* loved, no matter where they came from or end up.

And now, to wrap all this up, I'll let you in on my final secret: True heroes are *everywhere*, and sometimes they might even be *elsewhere*, but you can always find one *here* with just the right amount of magic.

Epilogue

Roll Right In…

Ezra Benjamin Castle of 23 Somerset Drive, Peckham finished tying the laces on his shiny new black Kickers. He stood up, straightened the tie around his neck, and looked in the hallway mirror.

'Well, don't you look smart,' beamed Mum as she smoothed out the lapels of his blazer. 'You got everything packed in your rucksack?'

Ezra reached down to pick up the giant rucksack full of all his new stationery, pencil case, PE kit, notepads, fidget toys, and more. It felt heavier than him as he pulled it over his shoulders.

'I think so,' he replied, shuffling the straps into a comfortable position.

'Here he is!' announced Dad as he flew down the stairs.

'Didn't want to miss the farewell before your first day of secondary school. Looking sharp, Ezra!' he smiled.

Mum and Dad looked down at Ezra standing there with his brand new uniform and slightly worried expression.

'We're proud of you,' said Mum, reaching forward and giving him a hug. 'You knock 'em dead!'

As Mum moved away from the hug and Ezra took hold of the front door, he was feeling all sorts of things. It had been a different kind of summer. A summer when he had felt more than ever that he was *somewhere*, at least for the most part. As he looked at Mum's face, he knew there was still a lot he didn't know how to do, but he was getting better at asking Mum and Dad to help him figure those things out.

Glancing down at his blazer and tie, his mind began to feel a bit like a jumbled-up whirlpool of whipped everything when, luckily, he was distracted by a memory. It was the memory of Uncle Leopold and the delicious, warm smell of scones in The Rolling Pin. Half a smile spread across Ezra's face and a tiny sliver of confidence tiptoed across the delicate new thread that had been sewn into his heart.

Roll right in, Ezra thought. *Roll right in…*

Author's Note

On the 31st March 2023, 83,840 children were in the care of local authorities in England alone. Of these 'looked-after' children, 45% have diagnosable mental health conditions, often in relation to adverse childhood experiences (ACEs) that have affected them. In the UK, there are around 6,000 looked-after children who need to be adopted each year.

According to the charity ADHD UK, around 2.6 million people in the UK have the disorder, but only 600,000 are formally diagnosed. Looked-after children are statistically more likely to have some kind of neurodivergence, with ADHD and ASD amongst the most common diagnoses, and this intersectionality can often make everyday life in a world primarily designed for neurotypical people a challenge to navigate.

When you next encounter an adopted and/or neurodivergent child who might be struggling with the demands of school or a club or a birthday party, for example, perhaps you might look at them through Ezra's eyes. As a parent with an atypical family myself, I know the benefit that this understanding and empathy can bring, however difficult it may be.

If you wish to find out more about adoption and related support in the UK, here are some links:

https://www.adoptionuk.org/

https://wearefamilyadoption.org.uk/

https://www.coramadoption.org.uk/

If you would like to learn more about ADHD, you could take a look at these sites to get you started:

https://adhduk.co.uk/about-adhd/

https://www.adhdfoundation.org.uk/resources/

https://www.youngminds.org.uk/parent/parents-a-z-mental-health-guide/adhd/

Acknowledgements

My love and thanks as always to A, J and M—J for whom I wrote this story first and foremost, M for her joyful humour and warmth, and A who takes care of us all and puts up with me still. Thanks to my family (on both sides) for their support, understanding, and encouragement over the years. Thanks are also owed to Blaze, my cockapoo, for inspiring the character of Parker, even if all that jumping up and licking can be a bit much sometimes…

Thanks to my early readers Giles, Nick, Benjamin, and Juliette for your input, and to Craig, John, and Cali at Dreamsphere Books for taking this little book on and giving it such warm, loving, and expert care.

Finally, a deep gratitude is owed to Juliette for the wonderful cover artwork and illustrations. It was fantastic to be able to work with you and see you bring Ezra to life, especially given your own unique insight into the nature of this story.

And thank you to you, dear reader, for trying to find your own somewhere, and for helping others to find theirs.

About the Author

R. D. Stevens grew up in Kent, England, with an overactive imagination and a love of big questions.

His award-winning YA debut, *The Journal*, was released by Vulpine Press in August '22, and *The Freeze*, his sophomore novel, was released in Jan '23. He has also had a range of other fiction and non-fiction published in various destinations. He was shortlisted for the Olga Sinclair Prize 2023, longlisted for the Aurora National Short Fiction Prize 2023, and has won awards for both his novels.

In 2023, he released a podcast 'Perspectives on Pages' which he co-hosts with fellow small press author Benjamin Roesch. He also works in collaboration with notforvanity.com as a guest reviewer of their indie author content.

Outside of writing, after spending fifteen years in secondary school teaching, he currently works at King's College University, delivers philosophy seminars to Sixth Formers, and loves to read books, play the guitar, and talk about existentialism (with anyone who'll listen). He lives in London with his atypical family and FOMO-suffering dog.

Ezra and the Great Bin Jah Meen is his third novel and first published with Dreamsphere Books.

Milton Keynes UK
Ingram Content Group UK Ltd.
UKHW041408211124
451419UK00013B/81

9 781998 055692